Other Books in the growing Faithgirlz!™ library

The Faithgirlz! Bible
NIV Faithgirlz! Backpack Bible
My Faithgirlz! Journal

Nonfiction

Everybody Tells Me to be Myself, but I Don't Know Who I Am

The Sophie Series

Sophie's World (Book One)
Sophie's Secret (Book Two)
Sophie and the Scoundrels (Book Three)
Sophie's Irish Showdown (Book Four)
Sophie's First Dance? (Book Five)
Sophie's Stormy Summer (Book Six)
Sophie Breaks the Code (Book Seven)
Sophie Flakes Out (Book Nine)
Sophie Loves Jimmy (Book Ten)
Sophie Loses the Lead (Book Eleven)
Sophie's Encore (Book Twelve)

Check out www.faithgirlz.com

faiThGirLz!™

beautyLAB

NancyRue

zonderkidz

ZONDERVAN.com/
AUTHORTRACKER
follow your favorite authors

The children's group of Zondervan

www.zonderkidz.com

Beauty Lab
Copyright © 2007 by Nancy Rue
Illustrations copyright © 2007 by Zondervan

Requests for information should be addressed to:
Zonderkidz, Grand Rapids, Michigan 49530

Library of Congress Cataloging-in-Publication Data

Rue, Nancy N.
   Beauty lab / by Nancy Rue.
         p. cm. — (Faithgirlz!)
   ISBN-13: 978-0-310-71276-3 (softcover)
   ISBN-10: 0-310-71276-9 (softcover)
   1. Grooming for girls — Juvenile literature. 2. Christian life —
Juvenile literature. 3. Beauty, Personal — Juvenile literature.
   I. Title.
   RA777.25.R84 2007
   646.7'042—dc22
                                                                   2006026235

Published in association with the literary agency of Alive Communications, Inc., 7680 Goddard
Street, Suite 200, Colorado Springs, CO 80920,
www.alivecommunications.com

Editor: Barbara Scott
Interior Design: Sherri L. Hoffman
Art Direction & Cover Design: Merit Alderink

Printed in the United States of America

07 08 09 10 11 12 • 10 9 8 7 6 5 4 3 2 1

Contents

Many thanks to the most beautiful young woman I know, my daughter Marijean Rue. Her hard work and wonderful ideas have helped shape this book. Her wisdom and love have shown me what real beauty is.

chapter one

You've Got It
GOIN' ON

The morning Betsy Honeycutt turned eleven, she took a big ol' long look in the mirror, and she didn't like what she saw.

That was pretty weird, since she had seen the very same face the day before (and the day before that and the day before — well, you get the idea), and she hadn't thought much about her freckles or her blue eyes or her honey-brown bob one way or the other. Yesterday she was just Betsy. But today — yikes!

Has my nose always been that long? she thought. *Gross! It looks like a fishhook!*

And what about my eyes? They've gotten closer together — I know they have!

Betsy watched her upper lip curl. Her very thin lip — not plump and luscious like the girls' mouths in the magazines that she'd just fanned across her bed. In fact, there was nothing about her that was even remotely like a model, or, come to think of it, like any of the girls at school that everybody was imitating. She narrowed her eyes at her reflection.

Her hair wasn't long and shiny and thick like Madison's.

Her teeth weren't perfectly white and straight like Taylor's.

And where in the *world* had that *zit* come from? Ashleigh didn't have *zits!*

Betsy gasped right out loud and shoved her face closer to the mirror. It was a pimple between her eyebrows, all right, red and ugly and growing bigger by the millisecond.

She stepped back, hoping it wouldn't look so hideous from farther away, but it was like there was a spotlight shining on it so the entire world could check it out. And not only that, but now she could see her whole self in all her glory.

"Uh, I am *so not* glorious," Betsy said.

The girl in the mirror looked to her like a shapeless blob, dressed in a too-small T-shirt and a too-big pair of shorts that revealed legs hairier than her cocker spaniel's. When she put her hand up to her mouth in disgust, all she saw was the froggy green nail polish she'd put on at last week's sleepover and had been steadily gnawing away at ever since.

"And this is before I turned the lights on," Betsy told the stranger-self. "EWWWWW!"

She turned away from the mirror and looked down at the clear-skinned faces of the perfect girls on the magazine covers. *Will I ever be that pretty?* she thought.

She didn't see how the answer could ever be yes.

Which of these comes closest to what you were you
thinking as you read Betsy's story?

    ___ I don't get it. I hardly ever hang out looking in the mirror.
    ___ Um, I kind of like what I see when I look in the mirror.
    ___ Hello-o! I know exactly how she feels!

Just about every girl between the ages of eight and twelve
starts to think—at least a little bit—about the way she looks. But
did you know that the minute you're aware that your appearance
is a big part of yourself, you're on a journey?

It can be a lifetime of visits to the mirror where you can
always find something *wrong.* Or . . . it can be an adventure of
discovering the true, absolute, no-denying-it beauty that every girl
has—that *you* have.

The choice is pretty much a no-brainer, which is why you have
this book in your hand. This book is here to help you set out on
the way-fun path to finding your beautiful self. And not just the
hair-and-skin-and-clothes outside self, but the unique, one-of-a-
kind inside you, which is where real beauty comes from. More on
that later.

Before you begin the adventure, it's good to know where
you are right now. Write in the space on the next page what you
would say to Betsy if you were in her bedroom, watching her
suffer in front of the mirror. Look back at what you checked off
above to help you. There are no right or wrong answers, so be
free and real as you write. If, as you read on in this book, you
change your mind about what you want to say to Betsy, you'll
have a chance to express that when we get to the end.

Dear Betsy...

When it comes to thinking about the way you look, you're probably somewhere between "What's a mirror?" and "I want to put a bag over my head!" Whatever you think about your beauty, chances are you've gotten some ideas about what beautiful is by looking around and listening. Maybe you've heard things like this:

> "She's so thin. I wish I looked like her."
> "Her skin is perfect. Look at that! I bet she's never had a pimple."
> "Long blonde hair and big blue eyes — now *that's* what I'm talking about."
> "Train to be a model or just look like one! Call now! Operators are standing by!"

To hear people talk, you'd think the only girls who could be considered beautiful are pencil skinny with flawless complexions, long blonde hair, and big blue eyes; and they dress only in the trends that just started this morning. But think about all the girls and women you know that you consider beautiful. Do they all look like that?

What about

* ❀ your best friend?
* ❀ your favorite female teacher?
* ❀ your cool aunt, the cousin you want to be like, and your mom?
* ❀ And, hey — what about *you*?

Yeah, you. If you counted up all the people who like you and love you, you'd run out of fingers. Ask any one of them if he or she thinks you're a beautiful person, and you'll hear, "Honey, you're drop-dead gorgeous," or something like that.

The point is, no matter what people say about being beautiful, when you get right down to it, the ones who count in your life know real, true, unique beauty when they see it. So how do girls get the idea that they have to look like the cover girl on *Seventeen* to be pretty?

Simple.

(Important Thing):
Don't ask a boy younger than twenty-five. He can't handle questions like that yet. You're sure to get a variation of, "Yeah, if you like baboons," which probably means he likes you — but don't even go there.

 From the media. That's TV, movies, billboards, magazines — anything that a lot of people see. The beauties there are all different, but they have one thing in common: they're perfect. Oops — wait. They *look* perfect. But if you met one of them outside the studio, you'd see right away that she has flaws just like everybody else: A piece of hair that won't stay out of her eye; the retainer she just popped in; maybe even a zit — yikes! You don't see those things in an ad or on the movie screen because (1) a team of makeup artists, personal trainers, and wardrobe consultants were all over her before she went before the camera, and (2) film editors can do amazing things with digital enhancing, just the way you can in Photoshop. A couple of clicks and that piece of flyaway hair or that enormous pimple disappears. The eyes are darker. The dress fits better. Get it? A famous model named Cindy Crawford once said, "Even I don't wake up looking like Cindy Crawford."

From models. You may have seen a professional model in person, and she did look pretty perfect to you. There wasn't an ounce of fat on her body! Before you consider yourself a hippo because at ten years old you weigh more than she does at twenty, remember this: A girl who becomes a model tends to be naturally thin and very tall to begin with. Then it becomes part of her job to keep her weight low so the curves of her body don't take attention away from the clothes she's modeling. Many models diet constantly, practically living on water and celery, and they work out daily for hours on end. Don't even think about doing that. You have healthy growing to do.

From what boys say. Like you care, right? But you can't help hearing them because they're so loud. They're going through their own stuff right now, so a lot of them think they have to be funny all the time. You've probably noticed that what boys consider funny is different from what cracks up you and your friends. They think it's hilarious to call you Tinsel Teeth because you just got braces or to swat at cooties when you stand next to them. Even though you know they're just being absurd little creeps, you can get your feelings hurt. Give them a few years. They'll get nicer. Meanwhile, don't take beauty tips from them.

By comparing yourself to the "cool" girls. Sometime in elementary school, it starts to become obvious that some girls are considered "cooler" than others. We don't know who decides that. Unfortunately, it just happens. Because the cool girls get a lot of attention and have a bunch of friends, almost everybody wants to be like them. And then the comparing starts:

- "Her hair is blonder (or darker) than mine."
- "Her eyes are bigger (or bluer or sparklier) than mine."
- "My clothes aren't as cute as hers."
- "She doesn't have to wear stupid braces like I do."

It can be pretty tempting to try to change yourself to be more like the cool girl. Or you may dislike the cool girl because seeing her makes you feel so bad about yourself. Or — if you happen to be a cool girl — you may work overtime trying to *stay* cool. None of that is any fun. And none of it makes you beautiful. It makes you worried, unhappy, and resentful — but not beautiful.

Besides, here's the deal — and if you get nothing else from this book, get this — YOU ARE ALREADY BEAUTIFUL!!!! Maybe on the outside you haven't "grown into yourself" yet. Maybe you haven't learned to make the most of what you have. Maybe you have hard stuff going on in your life that keeps you from really showing your beauty. But you were made to be a beautiful person. She's in there. After all, God doesn't make ugly. Okay, so maybe roaches are ugly . . . but the boy roaches think they're kinda cute.

You were made to be your unique, shining, beautiful, true self. This journey you're on is about finding that self and letting her shine.

Who says? Well, hello-o . . .

GOT GOD?

You believe in God, right? You believe God's in charge because he's perfect, yes? So you agree that all the things David says about God in Psalm 139 are true:

God knows everything about you (vs. 1–4).
God is everywhere (vs. 5–12).
God created your "inmost being" (vs. 13).

If you believe that, then you can say this right along with David:

> "I praise you because I am fearfully and wonderfully made; your works are wonderful, I know that full well."
>
> —Psalm 139:14

Fearfully, by the way, doesn't mean like Frankenstein's monster (although even he turned out to have a soft spot). It means *awesomely*. You were made to be awesome and wonderful. There it is, right in the Bible. God knit you together with love in every stitch. He thought of you, and you *became*. And as David says, "How precious to me are your thoughts, O God!" (Psalm 139:17).

You are the result of God's precious thought. How cool is that! Not some modeling agency's thought (though there's nothing wrong with being a model), or a cool girl's thought (although a lot of cool girls are really nice), or that boy's thought (which he doesn't even understand himself!) — *God's* thought.

You are a beautiful person. Believe it.

God doesn't just want you to *know* you're beautiful. God wants you to *show* it — not by plastering on makeup or spending a bajillion dollars on clothes, but by shining from the inside. Jesus talked about that in his teaching.

You can — and should — let God's "precious thought" out where it can shine like a light. Be every bit the beauty God created you to be, so other people will see Christ in you and be drawn to you.

Then you can love them and show them more about God's works. No one can do that when she's hiding her beautiful self.

Okay . . . go ahead and ask it . . . You know you want to:

"But aren't some girls more precious than others? Don't some just naturally shine brighter?"

Okay, picture God creating a new baby girl. Imagine the God whose works are wonderful saying, "Oops, I didn't make little Megan as precious as baby Brittany. I hate it when that happens." Can you honestly imagine him saying that?

Uh . . . no. Every tiny being God creates has his beautiful fingerprints on her. She's shaped with love and "breathed through" with her own gifts and special brightness. Each child is an original. Each one is God's art. Each is priceless.

And that includes you, Precious Thought. You are fearfully and wonderfully made. Your part is to uncover the beauty — inside and out. It's a journey. Are you ready to begin?

"No one lights a lamp and hides it in a jar or puts it under a bed. Instead, he puts it on a stand, so that those who come in can see the light." — Luke 8:16

There were women in the crowd when Jesus said this — Mary Magdalene, Joanna, Susanna, and many others who had been healed by Jesus and with their own money were helping to support him and his disciples. They listened to Jesus' message. So should you.

That Is SO Me

Start by being really honest with yourself. Complete this quiz alone or with a friend you totally trust. If you're afraid a curious younger bro or sis will get those little hands on this book, keep track of your answers on another piece of paper and make confetti out of it later. This is your very private stuff.

Put a star [*] next to each thought below that you've ever had for more than, like, two seconds. Even if you don't believe the thought, if it nags you sometimes, give it a star. There's no right or wrong. No good or bad. There's just you.

*_ I'm fat.

*_ I'm ugly. STD

*_ I don't look that bad except for my _forehead & nose_.

*_ I'm too tall (or short).

___ I have my father's _____ (ex: nose, lips), which is not good.

*_ I want to look like a star (model, singer, actress ...).

___ I'll never look like a star, which is depressing.

*_ Some people tell me I'm pretty, but I don't believe them. STD

*_ Some people tell me I'm not pretty, and I believe them. STD

*_ I don't do that much to look prettier, because it isn't gonna help. STD

*_ I wish I were cuter, so I'd have more friends.

___ I don't care about my appearance. I'm not the girly girl type.

___ It drives me nuts to have to wear _____ (ex: glasses, braces, a school uniform). They make me look lame.

Now count your stars and put your number here: (8)*'s

If you have between 11 and 13 stars, this book is SO for you. You seem to be having a tough time seeing your own beauty. This journey is going to be especially amazing for you, because every discovery will surprise you. You're going to love the real you.

If you have between 4 and 10 stars, you're not alone. Most girls your age go back and forth between thinking they're not so bad and deciding they're total freaks. But read on, and get a true picture of yourself that gets better all the time.

If you have between 0 and 3 stars, you're in a great place to have some fun with your beauty right from the start. As you read, be aware of the things you did star, because we're going to chase those thoughts away.

Whatever your score, you're about to set out on an expedition. You won't turn into a model (unless that's what God has in mind for you). You won't suddenly become like the "cool" girls. But you *will* find your own cool — the beautiful person you were made to be.

Whatever your score says is not about whether you're practically perfect or totally messed up. That goes for all the quizzes in this book. They're just a way to show you where you are and where you might be able to go. If you were perfect already (and nobody is!), you wouldn't have the adventure of the journey ahead of you.

You're Good to Go

It's time to pack your bags for the journey. Be sure to do the following Beauty Search before you move on to chapter two.

Beauty Search

With *Beauty Lab* and a pen or pencil, go to a mirror where you can see a lot of yourself. This works best if there's no one around who's going to tease you for gazing at your reflection.

Be honest about the beautiful things you see in the mirror. Look at every detail—your nice hairline; that cute little chicken pox scar; and your big, white, shiny teeth. Look at your hair, mouth, complexion, face shape, eyebrows, smile, eyes, chin, nose, arms, legs, height, shoulders, and hands. Describe those precious things. Again, be honest, but make sure everything you include is a compliment to you.

Look in the mirror again and smile at that girl as if you want to be her best friend. Check out what happens to your face.

Now stare at her as if you totally can't stand her.

Which face looked better?

This doesn't mean you have to grin 24/7. It means look for what you can like in people, which will make you smile. That's true beauty coming out of you. It also means be a best friend to yourself. Love *you* the way you do your BFF (best friend forever) and treat yourself as kindly. It looks good on you, girl!

> Being aware of your own loveliness so you can bring it out doesn't mean you think you're all that. Pointing it out to everyone in sight ("Do I not have the cutest freckles on my nose?") would be conceited, but that's not what we're doing here. So enjoy your beauty search.

In My Beauty Search, I Discovered That I Have...

hair

eyes

freckles

ears

lips

shoulders

arms

belly-button 😊

legs

curly toes 🐤

longish fingers

chapter two

The Skin
YOU'RE IN

Betsy dragged herself back to the mirror (after she scored an eleven on the quiz) and said about a hundred times, "I am fearfully and wonderfully made."

She actually *did* think her eyes were sparkling a little brighter than before. Her ears kind of stuck out, though. Madeline, her best friend, had nice, flat ears that didn't make her look like a Volkswagen with the doors open.

Oops, Betsy thought. *I'm not supposed to do that.*

She was actually getting better at not paying attention to the insults she gave herself, but it was still hard when other people threw them at her. Like that kid Jason ... When he asked her if that model of Mount St. Helens on her face was part of her science project, Betsy ran to the restroom in tears. She looked in the mirror and saw that Jason was wrong: There wasn't just *one* volcano-sized pimple about to erupt on her forehead, there were two! She was tempted to stick her head in one of the toilets and stay there.

But Betsy did what she was learning to do. She went to the people who really loved her and asked them, "Is it just me, or are these pimples the grossest things on the planet?"

Her father squinted at her and said, "What pimples?" Her mom told her not to worry about it, that she'd grow out of it.

She didn't mention when. Betsy's best friend said, "They're not that bad, really." Betsy loved her for lying.

None of those answers made Betsy feel any better. In fact, she even tried to get her mom to let her stay home from school the next day — and maybe the next and the next — until that science project on her face went away.

GOT GOD?

Even if your face isn't breaking out like Betsy's (and maybe it never will), taking care of your skin is a pretty huge thing, because your skin is the biggest organ your body has. It protects you, regulates your body temperature, and holds all the inner stuff in. If your skin isn't healthy, you can't be at your best, inside or out.

Since God wants you to be healthy, skin is a big thing to him too. Check out what happened to Job:

God told Satan that no matter what he did to Job, Job would never curse God. Satan took him up on the bet.

It didn't go as Satan expected. Even after Job had lost his oxen, donkeys, sheep, camels, and servants to various calamities—and all of his sons and daughters were killed when a house collapsed on them—he still didn't blame God.

So Satan said to God, "Skin for skin! ... A man will give all he has for his own life. But stretch out your hand and strike his flesh and bones, and he will surely curse you to your face" (Job 2:4–5). Satan had good reason to believe that. We human beings get very touchy about stuff happening to our bodies.

Notice that the worst thing Satan could think of was to cover Job's *skin* with painful sores—from the soles of his feet to the top of his head. He didn't give Job a series of bad hair days or grow his nose like Pinocchio. He went after that protective covering. There is something about skin funkiness that really freaks us out, partly because everybody can see it and some people don't hide the fact that it grosses them out.

So, yes, God understands how important our skin is to us. By the way, if you want the gory details about Job's skin condition, you can read about that in the book of Job. You can also read other mentions of skin care in the Bible and see that skin care is a symbol for God's love. Here are a couple of examples:

✦ Oil, which is one of the fruits of God's work, makes a person's face shine (Psalm 104:15).

✦ The woman in Bethany poured a whole container of perfume over Jesus' body as an act of devotion, a way of showing lavish love for God (Matthew 26:6–13).

✦ Keeping the skin clean was *really* a big deal for God's people. Ya think? In Leviticus, Moses spends four chapters (chapters 11–15) giving instructions for keeping clean!

✦ They were still at it in Jesus' time: "The Pharisees and all the Jews do not eat unless they give their hands a ceremonial washing, holding to the tradition of the elders. When they come from the marketplace they do not eat unless they wash" (Mark 7:3–4). This behavior was more about being clean inside than outside, but the tradition really helped them understand about being pure for God.

✦ And when someone actually had a close encounter with God, the person's face (skin) literally shone—like the sun. That happened to Moses (Exodus 34:29–30) and to Jesus (Matthew 17:2). It can even happen to you. When you truly believe in God's love, as Jesus showed it to us, you can "arise, shine, for your light has come" (Isaiah 60:1).

Here's the Deal

Like everything else God gives you, your skin needs to be taken care of. *Now* is the time to start, even if you haven't seen even a hint of a blemish. (That's a ladylike word for *zit*. It doesn't quite describe it, does it?)

Stuff You Totally Need to Know

🌸 Wash your face morning and night—and any other time you've worked up a sweat—with a gentle soap that contains NO acids. Rinse with at least fifteen splashes. Your skin won't shine if it still has soap on it. To block dirt, make the last few splashes cold water.

🌸 After you wash your face, smile. If your skin feels tight, put on a water-based liquid moisturizer that contains sunscreen. (We'll talk about that more below.)

Don't scrub like you would the bottom of a pot! Be gentle or you'll irritate your skin. Be sweet to yourself!

🌸 If your skin's really oily (you'll find that out below), use an oil-control lotion instead of moisturizer. That should have sunscreen in it too.

🌸 Don't forget the rest of your skin. Take regular showers or baths and wash with gentle soap, using a loofah or a wash-cloth so you can get rid of dead skin cells that naturally hang out. There are some really fun loofahs in stores these days with everything from frogs to rock stars on them. In the shower, pay attention to the following areas:

* neck — Dirt can gather in the little folds.
* arms — The skin on the backs of arms tends to get dry.
* elbows — A lot of people get really dark elbows, which are not attractive.
* buns — Pimples love to break out there.
* legs — Especially if you're really active, knees can get smudgy.
* feet — Obviously! Be sure to get in between toes where fungus likes to grow.

Rinse big-time, and when you get out of the shower or tub, use body lotion all over — you'll smell great and feel smooth. If that sounds like too much trouble, put some baby oil in a plastic spray bottle and squirt it on yourself while you're still wet. Then pat yourself dry with a towel. Don't rub, or it will all come off.

Make your skin-care routine as automatic as brushing your teeth. (We're hoping you're doing *that* regularly!)

Don't flop into bed at night without washing your face. It's carrying all the dirt and grime you've been exposed to all day. Yuck! If you're way tired when bedtime rolls around, ask your mom to get you some facial wipes. They're fast to use and will get you under the covers sooner.

More Stuff You Totally Need to Know

🌸 The sun's rays are great for giving you vitamins and keeping you in a good mood, but they aren't so great for your skin. No matter what anybody tells you, *a tan is not healthy!* It means you've damaged your skin.

🌸 Protect yourself now. When you're out in the sun soaking up vitamins between the hours of ten a.m. and four p.m., wear sunscreen with an SPF (sun protection factor) of at least 15 — higher if you have really fair skin — even if it's a cloudy day. Read the label to be sure it's no more than a year old — its effects do expire — and that it protects from both UVA and UBA rays.

🌸 Use it on every part of your body that's exposed, including your hands. Reapply it every two to three hours and after you've been in the water. Use SPF 15 lip balm on your lips too, since that thin skin burns easily.

> Tanning beds are no safer than the sun. Instead of planning a lifetime membership at a tanning salon for your future, start getting used to the idea that your natural skin color is beautiful too, because, hello-o, it's healthy!

It seems like a pain in the neck when you're at the beach or pool having a blast, but the kind of sun damage that causes cancer usually happens before a girl is twenty years old. In fact, getting two major sunburns before age eighteen doubles your chances of getting skin cancer in your life. You don't want skin cancer. Besides, as you get older, too-tanned skin will start to look like somebody's old leather handbag.

Eat healthy food. Make sure you get veggies, fruits, whole grains, lean protein (like chicken and fish), and some dairy products. Treats are fine, but don't overdo; savor something small and exquisite rather than devouring an entire bag of chips in front of the TV. The reason? Good food has the nutrients you need for beautiful skin. The nutrients repair skin when it gets damaged (which is constantly happening in tiny ways). Your skin has to be healthy to be pretty. Sodas and candy bars will not make you pretty. Believe it or not, broccoli will!

Try eating only foods whose ingredients you can pronounce. For example, apple, versus monotyri-pigrossolate sodium phosphate.

Drink a lot of water, like, at least eight 8-ounce glasses a day. If that's hard to do when you're in school, try to grab a couple of swallows every time you pass the water fountain to flush out the icky stuff you take in just by breathing. Water inside gives your skin a nice glow outside.

Get the kind of exercise that makes you sweat, so that your skin is naturally cleansed. Doing some activity that you really dig for twenty minutes a day will perk your skin — and you — right up. So come on ... Off the couch! Walk the dog, get a game of screaming hide-and-seek going with your friends, practice all the cheers you know—whatever gets a smile on your face and a flush in your cheeks.

Get at least eight to ten hours of sleep every night. While you're getting your ZZZZs, your body is busy restoring itself after everything it's been through all day—and that means your skin too.

FAQs
about Pimples

Q Where do pimples even come from?

A The closer you get to being a teenager, the more oil your body produces. In some girls, the oil glands really get going, and that can cause clogs of dead cells and oil that get infected. Presto—pimples.

Q Don't foods like french fries and chocolate cause zits?

A Nah. It's oil on the inside that makes skin break out. It may be, though, that white flour and sugar can make pimple problems worse, so healthy eating habits are always a good idea.

Q So how do I keep from getting them?

A The bad news is, sometimes you're going to get a pimple no matter what you do. Some people are more likely to get them because of the amount of oil they produce. Bummer. But you can prevent some breakouts by following the skin-care routine we've talked about.

Q If I get one of those evil ones that's all white and gross-looking, should I pop it?

A No! Sit on your hands if you have to but don't touch that zit. If you pop it or even pick at it, you'll spread the bacteria that has caused the infection, and more pimples just like that one are guaranteed to show up. The more you touch it, the longer it will take for it to heal. Besides, you could end up with a scar that'll be there forever. The pimple itself will go away — although the rest of the *day* may seem like forever.

Q Then what CAN I do? It's ugly!

A There are several things you can try on a pimple with a white head:

- Dab some tea tree oil on the spot with a cotton swab.

- Before you go to bed, put hot (not boiling!) water on the corner of a cloth and press it very gently on the pimple. Be patient, and it will open up and drain itself

- The next day, cover it up with a dab of a blemish stick.

Q What about those black plugs of dirt that get in my pores?

A Ah, yes, blackheads. They aren't dirt — they're skin pigment. They're created when oil and dead cells clog up a pore. They aren't infected yet, so those you can "operate on." After a hot shower, squeeze VERY gently with a finger on each side of the blackhead. Don't dig in with your fingernails, of course. If it

Your pimples always look bigger, redder, and yuckier to you than they do to anybody else. Don't remind everybody that you have them with loud wails of, "I hate my skin. I look like a pizza!" Remember, that little zit can't talk, so it says absolutely nothing about who you are.

doesn't pop out right away, leave it alone until the next time you take a shower. If you get a lot of blackheads, use a facial scrub when you wash. Rub it in with a washcloth or loofah. Be sure to be sweet with your skin while you're doing it. The grains in the scrub will do the work so you don't have to rub hard.

Q You're talking about a pimple or two. My face looks like I have big ol' boils. It even hurts. What do I do?

A That's a condition called *acne*, and it is a skin disease (though it's not catchy). The cause is complicated, but it has to do with hormones that are produced in the teen years which tell your body to produce more oil. In some people—and we don't know why—the oil gets stuck in the glands and plugs them up. The result is a face full of cysts and blackheads and pimples. Many times even after acne clears up, it leaves scars. Acne usually requires special care by a skin doctor (a dermatologist). You shouldn't have to suffer the pain. And no matter how beautiful you know you are on the inside, it's hard to feel pretty when your skin is sick. A dermatologist will tell you how to take care of your special skin and will probably prescribe medication in lotion and pill form to clear things up. You'll feel so much better. (If your mom says you'll just grow out of your acne, please show her this book.)

If you have dark skin, your skin will tend to scar easily. Don't squeeze a pimple no matter what.

That Is SO Me

Your skin is as unique as the rest of you, but you do belong to a skin *type*. Identifying your skin type can help you take extra-personalized care of You. Check out this quiz, and then be prepared to read the labels on the facial cleansers at the store.

Skin Type Quiz

Follow the flowchart on the next page to identify your skin type.

Tear a Kleenex into four small pieces. Before you wash your face in the morning, stick one piece on your forehead, one on a cheek, one on the side of your nose, and one on your chin. Keep the tissue on your face for about a minute.

If your skin gets red patches that look like a rash when you use skin-care products, you probably have <u>sensitive skin</u>. You can use products that are labeled "sensitive skin" or "hypoallergenic," or you can just avoid products that have fragrance in them. Be extra gentle with sensitive skin.

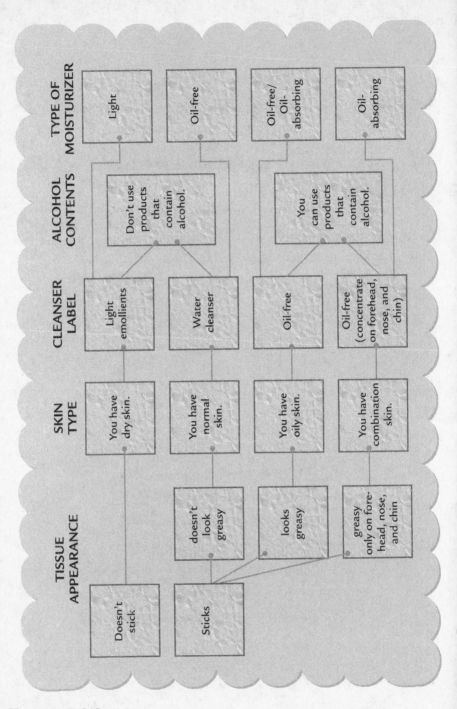

TYPE OF MOISTURIZER

- Light
- Oil-free
- Oil-free/Oil-absorbing
- Oil-absorbing

ALCOHOL CONTENTS

- Don't use products that contain alcohol.
- You can use products that contain alcohol.

CLEANSER LABEL

- Light emollients
- Water cleanser
- Oil-free
- Oil-free (concentrate on forehead, nose, and chin)

SKIN TYPE

- You have dry skin.
- You have normal skin.
- You have oily skin.
- You have combination skin.

TISSUE APPEARANCE

- Doesn't stick
- Sticks
- doesn't look greasy
- looks greasy
- greasy only on forehead, nose, and chin

Okay, so what about makeup? It could be you haven't thought about it yet. Or you may already be telling your mom that everybody else in your class is wearing it — why can't you? Or you might fall somewhere in between. Wherever you are with the idea of blush and lip gloss and eye shadow, answers to the cosmetics questions will help you be Your Most Beautiful You at this point in your life.

When

Some girls are lingering over the lipstick displays at age eight, while others can't see the point of it even when they're teenagers. If you're younger than twelve, it's better — for the sake of your still-delicate skin — to wait to put on makeup for real. (Though you can sure have fun playing around with it — more on that later.) At around twelve, if you're dying to use makeup, talk (calmly!) to your parents about it. They have the final word. (So no sneaking on eye shadow in the girls' bathroom if their final word is "not yet.")

Why Not

Makeup can make you look older than you are. It can make you feel grown-up. But if you *aren't* older, and you *aren't* grown-up, then you're not being your true self, are you? Being real is the best beauty treatment of all. (And walking around with a scowl on your face because your dad says no to makeup will NOT be a good look for you.)

If you do wear makeup, even playing around, always, always wash it off before you go to bed. Otherwise, it can plug up your pores while you sleep. Uh, nasty!

How Much

If you and your parents agree that a little makeup would be okay, you'll still want to be "the best You at your age." You aren't trying to cover anything up or create something that isn't there, so your best look will be sheer lip colors and glosses, a little natural-looking mascara, and some blush that's the color of your skin when you exercise. That will bring out your natural beauty, and that's what makeup is always supposed to do.

How

Before you wear makeup outside your house, have someone show you how to apply it. Don't ask somebody who seems to put on her own makeup with a putty knife (or without a mirror!).

Where

You might want to start with some pretty lip gloss on special occasions. Maybe from there you could wear it on the weekends, when you and your friends are getting together—that kind of thing. Whether you break out the lip color and blush for school depends on school rules, your parents' guidelines, and how much attention you want to pay to your mirror when you have stuff to do.

What If

You really want to wear makeup and your parents won't let you. Use lip balm, which not only keeps your lips healthy but also makes them feel like you have lipstick on. Put some petroleum jelly on the tips of your eyelashes to make them look darker and longer (just don't get it in your eyes). While you're waiting for the day to come when you'll have a whole collection of shadows and blushes and other fun things in your makeup case, take great care of your skin, be your best self, and remember that you are already beautiful. Let makeup just be something fun to look forward to.

You're Good to Go

Let's have some fun with this skin thing, because being beautiful is always supposed to be fun! One or more of these activities will get you glowing and feeling like your prettiest self.

Spa Night

Do this with your mom (or another special lady if there's no mom in your life). It might even be fun to invite a friend and her mom to join you. Gather your supplies (see lists below) and set up a place where you won't be interrupted by teasing brothers, curious fathers, etc. Your mom's bedroom and bathroom are ideal, but even the kitchen will work. Make it as special as you want with candles, flowers, pretty towels, and favorite music.

Give yourselves head-to-toe spa care. These are suggestions, but you can come up with your own if you want.

HAIR — Put a deep conditioner in your hair and wrap your head in plastic wrap. Try the one under "You're Good to Go" at the end of this chapter.

FACE — Try this fun facial mask:
Ingredients: 1 cup uncooked oats, ½ cup plain yogurt, 2 tablespoons honey

Instructions: Put all the ingredients in a blender and puree. Spread the mixture on your face in an even layer and let it dry for five minutes. Wash it off with warm water and pat dry with a clean towel. Store the extra mixture in the fridge in an air-tight container for up to two weeks. You can repeat this once a day (though no more). See if you can do it once a week.

HANDS — Soak your fingers in a bowl of warm, sudsy water and your feet in a soup pot full of the same. Get some good girl talking done or listen to music.

You'll need a bowl big enough for your hands, a pot big enough for your feet, warm water, and very mild liquid soap (the best kind is made from natural ingredients).

After you rinse and style your hair, file your fingernails and toenails and maybe paint them. Then enjoy a snack feast together. Be sure it's something healthy like smoothies.

Don't forget to take pictures!

Makeup Madness

Do this with your best friend or a group of BFFs. If you don't have close buds yet, this would be a great time to invite some girls you'd like to get to know.

Ask everyone to bring any makeup that can be put on with fingers or cotton swabs. Eye shadow applicators, mascara brushes, and eyeliner used by other people carry bacteria you don't need to share. Lipstick is the exception, since that can be wiped off with a tissue. Ask your friends to bring stand-up mirrors if they have them too.

You supply lots of tissue, washcloths, cotton swabs, towels, mirrors for those who don't have them, hair thingies (for getting hair out of faces), and magazines with pix of girls in cool (or bizarre!) makeup.

Set up a place where you can spread out, get the giggles, and be able to clean up if you accidentally spill something.

Anything goes as you do makeovers on each other. Try on different looks. Experiment with techniques. Laugh. Tell each other you're gorgeous. Take pictures.

Then wash it all off and snuggle in with a healthy snack (and maybe your all-time favorite BFF movie).

Go back to your natural self with memories of fun and a glimpse of what you might look like when it IS time for sophisticated makeup.

What I've Learned About the Skin I'm in ...

chapter three

Love
THE DO

B etsy stared — in horror — at the face that grinned at her through the window in the envelope. It was her worst school picture yet.

"Let's see yours!" Taylor said.

Betsy shoved the picture envelope into her binder and said, "No way. I look like a freak." By then Betsy's other friends had crowded around.

"Come on, Bets," Ashleigh said. "It can't be any worse than mine."

"Yes it can," Betsy said.

Ashleigh rolled her eyes and pulled out Betsy's packet. She looked at it for a minute and then turned to Taylor. "She's right," she said. "It IS worse."

Madison peered at it over Ashleigh's shoulder. "It's just your hair. It was doing something weird that day."

Taylor nodded. "You don't usually look like that, Bets. Really."

Betsy snatched the envelope back and waited for her friends to scatter before she sneaked another peek at herself.

"I am fearfully and wonderfully made," she said to her picture. "For a squirrel!"

Here's the Deal

Okay, so Betsy still has a long way to go on the find-your-own-beauty trail, but we hope YOU are convinced that every girl can have hair that's great for her. Let's start with some basics.

The Mane Things

Hair looks best when it's clean, so wash your hair as soon as it gets the least bit stringy. Don't wait 'til it's matted to your head, especially if your hair is becoming oily these days—which happens naturally as you grow toward teenager-hood.

Use the right kind of shampoo for your hair.

* Dry hair (especially coarse or curly)—moisturizing shampoo; baby shampoo if you wash your hair every day
* Oily hair (greasy when you skip a day of washing)—clarifying shampoo
* Normal hair (soft but not greasy)—shampoo for normal hair

It's okay to wash your hair every day, especially if it is oily or you do sports. Just get an empty shampoo bottle and fill it halfway with your shampoo and the rest of the way with warm water. Most shampoos are too strong to use everyday. Remember, you're being gentle with your beauty.

We say we're washing our hair, but we're really washing our head. Put a quarter-size glob of shampoo in the palm of your hand and work it into your wet scalp. Don't scratch with your fingernails, though. Use the pads of your fingers and massage. Enjoy. Even if you aren't a "girly" girl (like maybe your mom has to threaten you with grounding to get you to take a shower), washing your hair can still be fun. Remember when as a kid you made bunny ears with your lathered-up hair in the bathtub? Who says you can't still do that?

When you rinse, your hair will get the benefits of the shampoo. Unless you use a lot of "stuff" on your hair (mousse, gel, hairspray), you don't have to worry about the ends of your hair.

Rinse for two or three minutes. Really. If you leave shampoo in your hair, it won't shine. It's tempting to hurry to be done so you can play with your Game Boy or talk on the phone to your BFF. But let hair-washing time be your good alone time.

You probably don't have to use conditioner unless your hair gets really tangled when you wash it (or if you use products like gel when you style). A tiny dollop the size of a dime is plenty. Just apply it to the tangled places. Too much conditioner can build up on your hair so it loses its shimmer.

Always comb wet hair. Brushing it can actually break it. If you have trouble with tangles, use a comb with really big, spread-out teeth and be slow and gentle. Getting beautiful should never be painful!

Brush your hair before you go to bed at night (only if it's not wet, of course). If you have oily hair, brushing will spread the oils around to the right places. If you have dry hair (which you might if your hair is really curly or coarse), it will bring out the natural oils. Even if you have "normal" hair, brushing it is great for your scalp. It's kind of a soothing thing to do while you're thinking your end-of-the-day thoughts or listening to somebody read—whatever you do before you check out for the night.

Brush or comb your hair anytime during the day when it gets out of control—like after soccer practice or after a math test when you've been winding it around your finger while you concentrate. Just keep a small nylon-bristle brush in your backpack, give your tresses a few strokes, and you're gorgeous.

Have your hair trimmed about every six weeks. It doesn't reproduce itself like your skin does, so the ends start to look damaged if they're not cut off. If your hair is long, taking off the funky ends

Since hair is a bunch of dead cells that build up into strands that come out of your head (and your arms, legs, and armpits — lovely, huh?), it's very fragile. As much fun as it is to style, perm, glitter, and braid your hair, remember to be gentle with it. Accept it for what it is instead of trying to turn it into something it can't be. It will be so much more beautiful if you're nice to it.

will make it look healthier. If it's short, a trim will keep the style neat and fun. If you're trying to let it get longer, regular trims will keep it looking good. Split ends are basically dead, so they won't grow. If your hair is healthy and clean, you're going to feel good about that. After all, you're taking care of one of the gifts God gave you. When you feel good, you look good. It just happens.

Stylin'

You can stop right here if you want. But what if you'd like to do more than just wash your hair and get regular trims? First, you'll want to discover a style that suits your face. (No, Betsy. That does not mean a style that covers it up!)

If you want to be like your friends who all wear ponytails everyday, go for it. That's okay. If, on the other hand, you want to try out something that's really you . . .

- ✦ Go back to the mirror, which hopefully is now becoming your friend.
- ✦ Pull your hair back so you can really see the shape of your face.
- ✦ On a piece of paper, draw the shape you see.

It could be
very round,
oval,
square or square-ish,
long-rectangular,
triangular, or
heart-shaped.

Love that shape. It's you!

These are some ideas for hairstyles for your special face shape:

Very round —You precious thing! Long and straight is good. Or maybe a little height on top (scrunchie, anyone?) with some shape at the sides (the rest of your hair covering your ears, perhaps). If you want your face to look even rounder, go for short and curly. You get to choose.

Oval —Have at it, girl! Any style looks great on you. How fun is that?

Square or square-ish —This means your jaw and your forehead are kind of even. You can look way classy with a face like yours. Just keep your haircut above or below your jawline. Chopped off right at your jawline or poofiness going on at the corners of your forehead won't be your very best looks.

Long-rectangular —You can really look dramatic if you want to, as long as you avoid piling your hair right at the top of your head or wearing it too long and straight. You'll look fabulous with something fun and full at the sides.

Triangular —Great face for having some fun with bangs and different angles (like a ponytail that's off-center). Smooth hair at your jawline is spectacular on you.

Heart-shaped—You're a walking valentine! Curls or something else soft at your jawline is made for you. Try not to go poofy on top, though.

Another thing to think about—if you're really into this hair thing—is the *texture* of your hair. This is what we mean by texture:

Straight and soft—Like, you could be in hot rollers the whole day and your hair will still be straight an hour after you take them out (if not sooner!).

Curly, maybe even frizzy—You know it if you have it!

Thick and coarse—It takes forever to dry after you wash it, and if left to its own devices, it will get bushy.

Thick and fine—You have a lot of hair, but it's really soft so it wants to lie down.

Don't even try to change the texture of your hair because it isn't going to happen. And why would you want it to? It's part of the beauty journey to discover what works—and go with it. SO . . .

Straight and soft? Try a bob, or wear your hair long and all one length.

Curly or frizzy? Have your hair cut in layers, not all one length.

Thick and coarse? Try different lengths in one style and wear it medium to long. A stylist can thin your hair with special styling shears—but not every time you get your hair cut.

Thick and fine? You'll look great with your hair all one length except for layers around your face—either very long or very short.

Your *ethnic background* is another thing to consider when you're talking hair. It's a huge part of being true to who you are.

If you're *Asian*, women all around you are probably suffering from hair-envy. (They should read this book, shouldn't they?) You are exquisite with a simple, straight cut. Don't ever let anyone talk you into getting a perm!

If you're *Latin American*, have a blast with your thick, shiny hair. You don't have to look for complicated haircuts because you're fabulous with shoulder-length or longer hair. And don't even think about changing the color.

If you're *African American*, you have so many choices. One of the coolest ones, if you get frustrated with your hair, is to slick it back, which shows off your wonderful face. Don't fight your hair. Be proud of your heritage.

If you blow-dry your hair every day (and especially if you use a curling iron, hot rollers, or a flat iron) towel dry your hair before you blow-dry. That will cut down on the time your hair is exposed to heat, which can make it brittle.

Special Hair Issues

There's never a reason to stress about your tresses, but if you want to look polished and your hair just won't cooperate, try these hints:

Does your naturally curly hair get the frizzies?

✳ Rub a little gel between your fingers and then run your fingers through your just-washed, wet hair. Comb your hair into place and let it air dry.

* Or if you want to blow it dry, use a diffuser—a cone shaped thing that goes over the end of your dryer. Once you're through, keep your hands out of your hair. Every time you touch it, it gets frizzier.
* Don't go outside in humid weather with damp hair.

Is your hair baby thin?

* Use a *volumizing* shampoo. It coats your hair and makes it look thicker.
* Don't use conditioner unless your hair really tangles, and then just use the tiniest bit.
* When you blow-dry, bend over at the waist, let your hair hang down, and blast away until it's almost dry. Then stand up straight and style it into place.

Do you wish your hair were another color?

* It's fun to think about, but just let your hair be its natural color for now. Once you start coloring it, you have to keep doing it unless you want funky roots. You have enough other fun stuff to do.
* Your hair may not stay the color it is. Most blondes, for example, get darker as they get older. Wait and see how it turns out.
* Because your hair is still pretty delicate at this age, eighteen is really the earliest you should consider doing any color treating. Even then, keep in mind that it's hard to keep artificially colored hair healthy unless you have it done professionally. Then you're talking some big bucks . . .

With all God has to do, do you think he really cares about your hair? People in the Bible sure seemed to think so.

"Do not cut the hair at the sides of your head or clip off the edges of your beard" (Leviticus 19:27) is written as part of God's message through Moses to the entire assembly of Israel on how to be holy. Some Orthodox Jewish men still follow that rule to show total obedience to God. You'll see them with ringlets in front of their ears.

In Numbers 6:5, God said that if a man or woman wanted to make a special vow (a period of special devotion to God), one of the requirements was to not cut his or her hair. You'd know a God-devoted person by the long do.

In the New Testament, Luke (Luke 7:44) tells us about a woman who washed Jesus' feet with her tears and dried them with her hair before she kissed them and poured perfume on them.

One of the most famous people in the Bible to keep long hair was Samson. His mother was told by an angel — before Samson was even born — not to cut his hair so he would be "set apart to God from [his] birth" (Judges 13:5). As long as Samson stayed completely devoted to God — and let his hair grow as a symbol of that — he had the power to lead the Israelites in their battles against the bad guys (the Philistines). If you want to read more, his story is in Judges, chapters 13 – 16 — but be aware that it's some pretty rough stuff.

Jesus was impressed by how deeply she loved him. You *would* have to love someone a lot to dry his wet feet with your own hair.

It's the same in the Bible and now. In Matthew 10:30, Jesus says, "And even the very hairs of your head are all numbered." That is how much you are worth to God. Even if people hate you because you stand up for him, Jesus said, "*not a hair of your head will perish*" (Luke 21:18). You don't think God cares about your hair — and every other tiny part of you?

At the same time, Peter warns us women not to get so focused on our hair that we forget about being beautiful on the inside. Your beauty, he writes in 1 Peter 3:4, "should be that of your inner self, the unfading beauty of a gentle and quiet spirit, which is of great worth in God's sight."

Yes, take care of every hair God counted and put on your head. Enjoy it. And match its beauty with your actions. You won't just be *that girl with the pretty long brown hair*. You'll be *that really friendly (or nice or fun or crazy-but-I-like-her) girl with the pretty long brown hair.*

You're Good to Go

Want to do something just for fun?? Try this conditioner recipe with friends, your sisters, or — best yet — your mom. You can do it alone too. Just be sure to ask adult permission first. It's a great conditioner that feels weird in a good way and leaves your hair super shiny.

Directions:

❖ Put 1 tablespoon of oil (olive oil or any vegetable oil) in a dish that's microwave safe. Microwave it for five seconds.

❖ Add one egg yolk (not the whole egg). Ask your mom how to separate the egg.

❖ Whisk until blended, using a whisk or a fork.

- ❖ Massage the mixture into your hair. We *told* you it was going to feel weird!
- ❖ Put on a shower cap or a plastic bag (not over your face, obviously!).
- ❖ Leave it on for twenty minutes. This is why it's fun to do it with other hair-happy people. This is a great time for a snack or for starting on the next activity — or both.
- ❖ Shampoo your hair and rinse well.

You will now have the shiniest hair *ever*.

Serious about Going for a New Hairstyle?

If you haven't done it already, go back and circle the suggestions for your face shape and hair texture on pages 43 – 45.

Look through magazines for girls your age and find pictures of hair styles like the ones suggested for your shape and texture. Decide if you like any of them.

After discussing it with your mom, take this book (and a picture if you found one) to the best stylist your family can afford — and that can even be your aunt who makes everybody's hair look great. Your dad's barber — maybe not.

Explain — or have whoever takes you explain — what you want and ask the stylist if he or she thinks it's a good choice. (If you're getting a really big change and you get nervous, you can always start with a good trim, then next time go shorter.)

If you end up with the worst haircut on the planet — at least to you — remember that hair grows back. Meanwhile, get out the barrettes or headbands or clips, and use this as a chance to experiment. Wearing a hat 24/7 is not an option, because if your hair is clean and you're smiling, you're still beautiful. Got that?

What I Discovered About My God-Made Head of Hair …

chapter four

Smooth
MOVES

Betsy had to admit she really liked her new do. Her dad even noticed it, and he was the type to fall over the furniture before he realized her mom had changed it around.

Okay, so that kid Jason in her class said her new hairstyle made her look like a space alien. Huh. He should talk, Mr. Combs His Hair with a Lawn Mower.

But one day in the shower, Betsy discovered some *other* hair. When she raised her arm to wash her armpit — with the green loofah that looked like a frog in a tutu — she noticed something she hadn't picked up on before.

Fuzz under her arm.

Where did THAT come from? she thought. *Am I turning into Ape Girl?*

With water still pouring down on her, Betsy examined the rest of her body. Yikes! Her legs looked hairier too. They'd always had kind of a blonde fuzziness, but now the little hairs were darker, and there were more of them.

"I'm not wearing a skirt today!" Betsy said to the loofah frog. "Not today — and maybe never again. I have hairy legs!"

That Is SO Me

ake a few minutes to figure out whether you're feeling furry, like Betsy. In EACH ROW of boxes below, put a check in the ONE that is MOST like you.

Underarm hair:
- ☐ None
- ☐ Light 'n' fuzzy
- ☐ Dark and thick

I get sweat on my shirt under my arms:
- ☐ Almost never
- ☐ When I'm way active
- ☐ Whenever I move! (almost)

Leg hair:
- ☐ Not much
- ☐ I can barely see it.
- ☐ A person across the the room can see it.

My hair 'tude:
- ☐ What body hair?
- ☐ It's not a big deal.
- ☐ I want it off!

Why I want to shave:
- ☐ I don't!
- ☐ Some of my friends do.
- ☐ I feel like an ape.

Time I spend on beauty:
- ☐ As little as possible
- ☐ The basics (almost) daily
- ☐ As much as I can

Count how many check marks you have.

Boxes on the left: _____

Boxes in the center: _____

Boxes on the right: _____

Where do you have the most checks?

If you had the most checks on the left side, you probably won't want to add shaving your legs and underarms to your beauty chart yet. Read on, though, because someday you might, and it's good to know what you're doing when you're handling a razor!

If you had the most checks in the center, you might not be up for shaving your legs yet, but it's a good idea to keep an eye on your underarms, especially if you sweat there. Hair in the pits tends to hold perspiration where it can get a little smelly. A less than lovely odor wafting from under your arms is definitely not beautiful. Read on and we'll show you how to take care of that—and your legs—when you're ready.

If you had the most checks on the right side, you may have been eyeing your dad's razor for some time, or you suddenly feel like a furry family pet. That means it's the right time to approach your mom about shaving. This chapter will tell you all the secrets of hair removal, so that once mom gives the okay, you're ready to de-fuzz.

Since taking off body hair involves a razor or a product with strong chemicals in it, you really need adult permission before you go for it. And know that once you start shaving or using a hair-removal cream or lotion, the hair you take off will grow back coarser and thicker. This means it will be important to <u>keep</u> doing it regularly, or you'll be prickly and stubbly. Just think carefully first about whether you want to add this one more thing to your routine.

Here's the Deal

Have permission to streamline your legs and/or under-arms? Sure you're ready to commit to regular "defurrings"? Then get ready to feel very womanly . . .

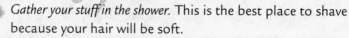

Shaving Directions

* *Gather your stuff in the shower.* This is the best place to shave because your hair will be soft.
  * Soap
  * Shaving cream (the thickest you can get your hands on). Ask if you can use your dad's the first time. The men's stuff is the best. If that's not available, use hair conditioner. (Shaving dry can give you a rash.)
  * A real razor with a clean blade. Disposable razors are harder to use on the bumps (like your knees). You'll be amazed at how easy it is to cut yourself and not even feel it at first. If you do use a disposable razor, throw it away after two or three times.

* *Wash the area you're going to shave with soap first.* Since shaving cream or hair conditioner isn't soap, it won't fight bacteria. Take care of that first.

* *Lather up.* It's really fun to cover your legs and underarms with rich, creamy shaving lather. Besides, it helps the hair stand up so the razor can catch it. Lather one underarm and shave it, then lather and shave the other, then one leg, then the other. Obviously, turn off the shower or step out of the water's stream while you're shaving or your lather will just go down the drain.

Shave. **Take your time!** Start at top of your armpit, and — pushing down VERY GENTLY with the razor — pull it toward the bottom in short strokes. As the shaving cream comes off, so will the hair. When shaving your legs, be sure you have a steady footing on a bathmat before propping the leg you're going to shave on the side of the bathtub or the ledge. Start at your ankle and work your way up in long, smooth strokes. Run the razor under the water when it gets goopy with shaving cream. Be extremely careful around bones that stick out. It helps to bend your knee before shaving it. Since the hair on your thighs is finer, lighter, and shorter, you don't usually have to shave them. Do not rush. Pay careful attention. If you need bandages when you get out of the shower, you were probably in too much of a hurry. Relax. This is *You* time.

Using a Hair Removal Product

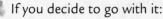

Decide if that's really what you want.

* A cream or lotion may sound safer than a razor blade, but it contains strong chemicals that irritate some people's skin. No one should use one if she has even the tiniest cut or scrape. It also takes longer than shaving, because you have to leave it on for five to ten minutes. If you plan to use it on your legs, that's going to take a lot, which gets expensive. Besides all that, it can smell funky.

If you decide to go with it:

* Read the directions very carefully and follow them exactly, including the part about testing a small area

first to see if it irritates your skin. After you use it, wash your hands thoroughly before you put them near your eyes or mouth. If you get some on anything but your legs or underarms, wash it off right away.

Other ways to take hair off:
* Laser — A professional can remove hair permanently. Sounds great, but it's way expensive and takes more time than you're going to want to spend.
* Waxing — Beauty salons will gladly use warm wax to remove your hair, but, man, does it hurt. Then you have to wait two weeks before you can have it done again, which can get pretty, well, hairy.

What about Eyebrows?

You probably haven't thought much about your eyebrows, unless

* you've found yourself with one big eyebrow going all the way across, or
* you really want a polished, finished look.

If you do want to take out stray hairs or get rid of your unibrow, follow these instructions very closely.

To make a space between eyebrows:
* Take a shower or wash your face with very warm water before you start. It won't sting as much when you pull the hairs out.
* Use good tweezers with slanted ends, not the pointy kind. Save those for splinters.
* Get close to the mirror. Better yet, use a hand mirror.

Eyebrows never grow all the way back once you pull them out. That means if you plucked all of yours out right now, you would hardly have eyebrows again. You may be thinking, <u>Why</u> <u>would</u> <u>I</u> <u>do</u> <u>THAT</u>? But you'd be surprised how easy it is to get carried away once you get hold of a pair of tweezers.

* Simply pinch a hair with the tweezers and give a sharp little tug. The hair should come right out.
* Don't tweeze your brows any further back than the inside corners of your eyes. If you get one eyebrow farther in than the other, don't try to even them out. You could end up with little commas for eyebrows.

 To make eyebrows look neat and groomed:
* Following the same guidelines as above, remove hairs that have popped in under your eyebrows
* Don't tweeze any above the brows at this point. It's too easy to wind up with thin lines instead of nice, velvety, healthy-looking eyebrows.
* Lots of women have their eyebrows waxed instead of tweezing them. Again, that hurts, and it costs money, and there's always the danger that too much eyebrow will be taken off. We advise you not to even go there right now.

GOT GOD?

The Bible doesn't have much to say about shaving. There's that one passage in Ezekiel where God told him, "Take a sharp sword and use it as a barber's razor to shave your head and beard" (Ezekiel 5:1). That doesn't exactly apply to you, since Ezekiel was being asked to do strange things to warn the people that they're about to go down. Do we need to even tell you not to attempt to shave your legs with a sword?

God doesn't talk about hair removal for women, because we girls didn't start going for the smooth look until it became proper for us to show our arms and legs in public, around the 1920s. Before that, what was the point? Now, being smooth and silky is considered part of good grooming for a woman in the United States. In some other countries, ladies skip the whole shaving thing and nobody bats an eye.

So basically, there's nothing bad about shaving or not shaving. It's really a matter of choice. Since your parents still have the final say in your choices, you'll have to go with theirs for a while. If your mom says you're too young to shave your legs, and you're feeling like Tarzan, try not to let it become a huge deal in your mind. Be responsible about the rest of your beauty care, and revisit the issue with Mom in a few months. A little maturity goes a long way. God *does* say something about that: "Honor your father and your mother, so that you may live long in the land the LORD your God is giving you" (Exodus 20:12).

It doesn't get much clearer than that!

You're Good to Go

The neat thing about having leg hair to shave — or even knowing you will someday — is that it means you're turning into a young woman. What better excuse for a celebration? In each of the following balloons, choose one or more details — or come up with your own.

Who to Invite:

Your best friend

Just you and your mom

A small circle of friends

A small assortment of females who enjoy being or becoming women

Where to Party

Any place without non-women!

Decorate to Create a Feeling of Fun Femininity

Flowers and butterflies

Women's sports memorabilia

Pictures of women you admire

Everything sparkly

What to Eat

Something no boy would be caught eating

The healthiest snacks everyone can create

Frilly desserts

Be sure to include just a little chocolate.

What to Do

Have a spa night (See chapter two).

Let everyone tell what she loves about being a girl.

Everyone brings a baby picture so you can guess who's who.

Squeal over how much everyone has changed.

Watch a special chick flick together.

Whatever creative, womanly ideas you come up with, have a wonderful time celebrating that God made you girls. Be sure to include some prayer time, because God will definitely be at your party.

What I Totally Love About Being a Mini-Woman ...

chapter five

Things That Will
COME IN HANDY
... AND FOOTY!

I f you know the answer, raise your hand," Mrs. Post, Betsy's teacher said.

Betsy knew it like she knew her own name, so she waved her arm in the air. In the desk in front of her, the new girl, Caroline, stuck her hand up too. And there they were: the prettiest shell-pink fingernails, shaped like little ovals on Caroline's long, smooth fingers.

Betsy pulled her arm down and inspected her own nails — what was left of them. She'd gnawed the last one down during that morning's math test. If they had a pop quiz in science, she planned to start chewing at the little pieces of skin that popped up around them. She decided it might be a good idea to wash her hands first, though, because there was a big old blue blob on her knuckle from the marker she'd used to color her toenails the night before when she was bored.

Suddenly, Betsy felt like all anybody could see were her chomped-off fingernails and scribbled-on toenails. She tucked her feet, which were in sandals, under her and hid her hands in her pockets. Mrs. Post called on Caroline for the right answer.

GOT GOD?

You might be wondering when poor Betsy is going to get it. Whether she's had a manicure or not shouldn't determine whether she raises her hand in class, right? Caroline sure isn't any smarter because she's wearing nail polish and doesn't have a marker blob on her index finger.

But the thing is, knowing her hands were looking pretty ragged *did* keep Betsy from showing what was really important—that she had studied, she was paying attention, and she wanted to participate because she knew she'd learn more that way. That's kind of a bummer.

It's even more of a bummer when you think about how many things God made our hands for:

Appealing to God for help—like Moses putting up his hands for God's power in battle (Exodus 17:11).

Healing—like Jesus laying hands on people to cure them (Mark 5:23), and the apostles doing it later (Acts 28:8).

Clapping—like people applauding for a new king (2 Kings 11:12).

Creating—as God's people have always done: Noah with the ark, Solomon's people with the temple, and Christians building up the church with their gifts (1 Corinthians 14:12).

Working—like the woman of noble character making clothes (Proverbs 31:24), and as Paul told the early Christians they should do (1 Thessalonians 4:11).

Helping— like that same noble woman who opens her arms to the poor and extends her hands to the needy (Proverbs 31:20)

Praying—as Paul told all Christians to do (1 Timothy 2:8).

If you stopped doing all of that because your hands didn't look like a nail-polish commercial, you'd really be letting God and yourself down. Since there are about a bajillion things you use your hands for, why not keep them looking at least clean and neat, if not downright fabulous?

That Is SO Me

When it comes to taking care of your hands, you can go from

Cleaner than your brother's	Basically clean and neat	A little polished (and clean and neat)	A funky expression of your wild self (and clean and neat)

Circle the look that you'd like to go for. Remember that there's no right or wrong. If you can't see yourself spending your birthday money on a bottle of Sparkling Scarlet, basically keeping your hands and nails clean is fine, even for the rest of your life. If you get really jazzed about drop-dead gorgeous nails, that's okay too.

Here's the Deal

No matter which of the four looks you circled, you'll need to follow the basics for taking care of your hands.

So here's the deal for hand health:

Wash your hands. Duh-uh, right? You'd be surprised how many people don't even think about it. Really clean your hands with warm water and soap (not just a quick run under the faucet before you take off). The bare minimum is to wash your hands when

* ❖ you've just used the bathroom;
* ❖ you're about to eat (whether it's sticking your hand in a bag of chips or sitting down to a big dinner);
* ❖ you're getting ready to fix something to eat;

- ❖ you've been touching an animal;
- ❖ you've been shopping;
- ❖ your hands feel sticky, greasy, grimy, or just a little icky;
- ❖ you have a cold (Wash your hands twice as much as usual and definitely after you've wiped your nose—hello-o!); and
- ❖ you've been around somebody who's sick.

This makes it sound like you have to have your hands in the sink all the time, but once it becomes a habit, you won't feel that way. It can be hard to get to soap and water when you're in school all day, so keep some hand sanitizer or wipes in your backpack. If somebody calls you a clean freak, pass him a Wet Wipe.

Get the dirt out from under your fingernails. Once a day, after you get out of the shower or tub, use a metal nail file (like the kind that comes on nail clippers) to gently scrape any left-over stuff from under your nails. Do it even if they don't look dirty. You'd be amazed what hides in there. (You don't really want to know . . .)

Even if you don't want glamour nails, it's way important to keep your hands clean. Since your fingers are into everything — all day long — they're the main way you pick up germs. No, you aren't picking them up between your fingertips, but they're constantly hitching a ride without your permission. Even if you can't see dirt, bacteria is there, ready to give you everything from a cold to . . . well, you get the idea.

Moisturize. Remember that from the skin chapter? When you're putting on lotion after your bath or shower, pay attention to your hands. This is especially important in cold climates where the temperatures can chap the skin on your hands just like it does your lips.

If, on *That Is SO Me*, you circled "Cleaner than your brother's," you're done.

Have a great day!

If you circled "Basically clean and neat," there are a few more steps. The good news is you don't have to do these every day. For hands and nails that say, "This girl takes good care of herself," do the following once a week:

File your nails with what's called an emery board. It's a nail file that has really fine sandpaper on it. Don't file with the metal thing, even though it's called a nail file. (Go figure!)

- Don't go back and forth like you're sawing a log. That's makes your nails weak. Start at one side of your nail and file in one direction toward the center, and then do the same from the other side.

- Since this takes time, you might do it while you're watching a movie or something.

- File until all your nails are the same length and shape, probably an oval or as close as you can get to that. You might have one or two nails that are nice and long and you're proud of them, but if the rest are way short, it's going to look funny. Say good-bye to the long ones and file away.

Take care of your cuticles. That's the skin around your nails that tends to creep onto them. It's healthier if they stay in place.

- Soak your fingers in a little bowl of hot, soapy water for a few minutes to soften up your cuticles.

Long nails look glamorous in magazines, but they probably aren't the best idea for you right now. They get in the way when you're writing, playing sports, or using the computer. They require a lot more attention. And they look as out of place when you're ten as three shades of eye shadow. Just above the tip of your finger is probably long enough. Shorter is okay too.

- Using what's called an orange stick (a little wooden thing with a slanted end), or a cotton swab, gently push the cuticles off your nails. Think of it as gently persuading them to get back where they belong.

- If any little pieces of cuticle stick up—like they're breaking off—you can clip them with tiny manicure scissors. Just to be on the safe side, have an experienced person (mom, big sister, etc.) show you how to do that. The broken cuticle is dead, but the skin that's still attached isn't. Nobody should bleed during a manicure!

That's it. Look at you. Nice hands, girlfriend!

If, on *That Is SO Me,* you circled "A little polished," you need to do all of the above before you move on to this part. Putting nail polish on nails that are dirty and ragged is sort of like putting frosting on a cake that hasn't been baked, you know? Once you're ready, here's what to do to look a little polished in the nail department.

Remove all old polish. You'll just need cotton balls you can dip in nail polish remover. Wipe from bottom to top until it ALL comes off.

Use a clear coat of polish first. There are special base coats, or you can just use clear. This is important if you plan to paint your nails a lot, because without it, colored polish can make them look yellow after a while.

Just use two or three strokes with the polish brush to cover your whole nail. That's all it takes. Any more and it gets gloppy. Let that dry before you move on. Don't rush. If that looks nice to you, you can stop there. Clear polish doesn't show as much when it chips off, and your nails will look shiny and pretty. If you want color . . .

Put on two layers of colored polish. Again, just use two or three strokes and let them dry completely in between. Instead of shaking the bottle to mix polish, roll it between your palms a couple of times. That away you won't get bubbles on your nails.

Apply a clear coat over that. That will help keep the color from chipping.

It only makes sense that if remover can take off nail polish, it can also take the finish off your mom's table or the color out of your jeans. Be sure you have everything covered. And do we need to mention not to get it even close to your eyes or mouth or anybody else's?

A lot of girls your age (and older!) bite their nails. You probably don't mean to; it's just that you get a little nervous or bored and before you realize it, you're chewing away. If you want to stop, pay attention for a few days to _when_ you bite. Then, try to find a substitute for those times. If you nibble while you watch TV, take up knitting. If you tend to chow down when you're stressed out, keep a wad of Silly Putty handy to squeeze. Remember that those fingers in your mouth are feeding you germs.

Don't do anything "nail intensive" for several hours, which means you might want to do your manicure before you go to bed. Don't let water touch them. Even if you speed dry by putting your hands in the freezer for two minutes, all the coats won't be entirely dry for three hours. So if you don't go right to bed, at least don't finger paint, dig a hole, or enter a pie-eating contest!

When your polish starts to chip — and it will — remove it with nail polish remover. A flake of polish in the middle of each nail is definitely not a good look for anybody. Not a good idea to chip it off with your other nails — or (Yikes!) with your teeth. Wait until you have time to sit down with remover and cotton balls.

If on *That Is SO Me*, you circled "A funky expression of your wild self," do ALL of the above, except that when you get ready to polish, use your imagination! This is one form of makeup parents don't usually object to (although you'll want to check with yours first), and it can be a blast.

Find fun colors you like. Nail polish can be pretty cheap to buy, and a bottle lasts a while. There are so many shades that come in everything from satiny to sparkly-like-metal. There's even glitter polish, which is TOO fun. Enjoy wild, strange nail color now, because as you get older, it won't always be the thing to do.

Avoid fake nails. You know—the kind you can buy in a package that you stick on with glue? That sticky stuff really isn't good for your nails. Who wants to look fake anyway, unless you're playing the wicked witch in the school play?

GOT GOD?

Hands are one thing—but why would God care about your feet? Nobody can see them most of the time; so, when it comes right down to it, why should *you* care that much about your feet?

Let's start with God, whose people talk about feet all the time in the Bible. Most of the time, they used them as symbols. That's when an object you can see—such as a cross—helps you understand something you can't see—like faith in God. In spite of their smelliness and fuzz between the toes, feet are important symbols in God's Word (which just goes to show God can use anybody and anything).

Feet are symbols for our ability to stand up for what's right.

"He set my feet on a rock and gave me a firm place to stand." —PSALM 40:2

"For you have delivered me from death and my feet from stumbling." —PSALM 56:13

There are lots of symbols of walking a path with God.

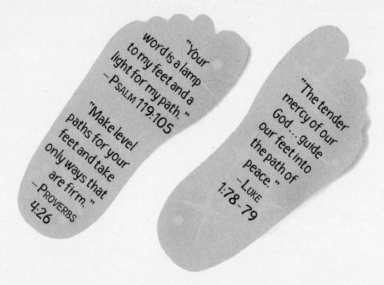

"Your word is a lamp to my feet and a light for my path."
— PSALM 119:105

"Make level paths for your feet and take only ways that are firm."
— PROVERBS 4:26

"The tender mercy of our God ...guide our feet into the path of peace."
— LUKE 1:78-79

Jesus washed the disciples' feet to symbolize how selfless God's love is, and how we have to love each other the same way.

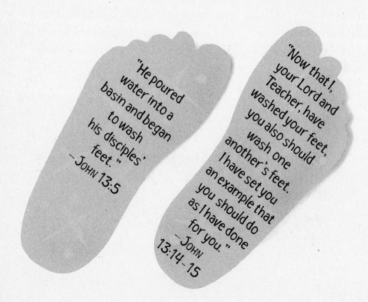

"He poured water into a basin and began to wash his disciples' feet."
— JOHN 13:5

"Now that I, your Lord and Teacher, have washed your feet, you also should wash one another's feet. I have set you an example that you should do as I have done for you."
— JOHN 13:14-15

You basically take care of your feet the same way you do your hands, with just a few special variations.

- ✣ Since toenails are tougher than fingernails, trim them with clippers instead of trying to file them.
- ✣ It's better to cut your toenails straight across instead of making ovals. Otherwise, you can get ingrown toenails. Ouch!
- ✣ While you're doing your weekly manicure, soak your feet in warm water to soften them up.
- ✣ Then use the pointed thing on the nail clippers to clean out the dirt from under your toenails. You think your *fingernails* get icky ...
- ✣ If you're going to polish your toenails, put pieces of cotton between your toes to spread them out. That way you won't get polish all over them.

Foot Funkiness

Warts. It's common to get them on your hands too. Although they're not anybody's best look, they're harmless and usually go away. You can try treatments from the drug store, but know that it takes a while for them to shrivel up. If a wart is really bugging you, especially if it's on the bottom of your foot (a plantar wart) a doctor can "freeze" it off. And by the way, frogs and toads don't give you warts, so don't run screaming from them.

Pee-yew! Yeah, feet can definitely get smelly. Once they do, you have to wash them to get rid of the stinkiness. Here are tips to prevent them from smelling up the place to begin with:

- Wear socks made of natural fibers, like cotton or wool, that absorb sweat before it causes yuckiness.
- Your shoes should be made of natural stuff too, such as leather or canvas. Plastic tennies and sandals may be fun, but, ooh, can they smell!
- If your shoes are giving off a less-than-delicious aroma, sprinkle baking soda inside them and leave it overnight.
- Sneakers cause more of a stench than any other kind of shoe. If you have a big problem with stinky feet, switch to sandals or loafers or cute flats when you can.

If your feet are suddenly bigger than your mom's, even though you're only eleven or so, don't freak. Women's feet are commonly larger now than they were even a generation ago. There's nothing wrong with big feet. Some of the most beautiful women in the world have slipped into a size nine or larger.

Hurting feet. If you get blisters or you can't wait to take your shoes off, you're probably wearing shoes that don't fit well. Your feet are growing right now, so have your feet measured every time you go shopping for shoes. And don't beg for the pair you love if the store doesn't have your size.

You want higher heels, but your mom won't let you. You know what? You need to listen to her. In the first place, three-inch heels when you're ten are right up there with the glamour nails and the heavy eye shadow we've been talking about. You're going to look like you're playing dress up with your mom's shoes. And most important of all, high heels throw your spine completely out of line and cause all kinds of problems with hips, knees, and even necks. They're cool for special occasions as you get older, but never for all day. Be part of the generation that says, "We will NOT walk around on stilts! We will take care of our bodies!"

Between-the-toe fungus. Red, scaly patches? That's called athlete's foot, though you don't have to be an athlete to get it. To avoid it, wear flip-flops when you take a shower in a locker room or at a pool, since that's where we usually pick up the fungus. Dry your feet really well after a bath, and don't wear the same shoes all the time. If you do get athlete's foot, start treating it with a powder, spray, or cream you can get at the drugstore. It won't go away by itself, and who wants itchy feet 24/7?

You're Good to Go

By this time you might be thinking that doing the beauty thing is a lot of work. You've got your hair to take care of. Your skin. Your hands. Even your toenails. Yikes! How are you even supposed to remember all that stuff, much less do it?

What do you say we stop and take care of that right now? How about making a Beauty Chart to help you keep track of what to do and when?

What You'll Need:

+ a piece of poster board, poster-sized paper, or four sheets of regular paper taped together to make one big square
+ a yardstick or ruler
+ a pencil
+ markers, colored pencils, or crayons
+ anything else you want to use to decorate your chart—stickers, stars, pictures from magazines, even photos of you doing your beauty-care thing
+ tacks or that gummy stuff you use to hang posters

How to Do It

There is no right or wrong way for your chart to look, so be creative. It should include the following steps.

(The ones with stars beside them are the optional items. Include those on your chart only if you're really into them.)

Write these down the left side:

EVERY DAY
wash body
wash hair
*use conditioner
*shave legs and pits

comb wet hair
use body lotion
clean under fingernails
drink eight glasses water
get thirty minutes exercise
wash hands often

EVERY MORNING
wash face
use moisturizer with sunscreen
brush hair
*style hair

EVERY NIGHT
wash face
use moisturizer
brush hair
get eight hours sleep

WEEKLY
soak feet
*remove old nail polish
file nails
take care of cuticles
clean under toenails
clip toenails
*put on new polish

EVERY SIX WEEKS
have hair trimmed

If you live in a house where anything you display is fair game for brothers and sisters — or you just want to be more private — you can make a smaller chart in a notebook, maybe a special beauty journal, or the place you keep all your other personal writings. Make the chart the same way as described below, only in miniature.

Across the top, write two months worth of dates, so that you form columns for checking things off. (You've seen charts like this in school a bunch, right?)

Using your ruler or yardstick, draw lines across for each item and down for each date, making boxes. Decorate your chart however you want to.

Find a good place to hang your chart so you'll remember to check items off each day/week.

You can make check marks with a cool pen or marker, or you can use stars, stickers, or smiley faces—whatever makes it fun for you to keep track of what good care you are taking of yourself.

It's very cool to watch yourself form habits. Remember though, that if you miss a day doing one of your beauty tasks, it doesn't mean you're going to be ugly that day. Just get back on track tomorrow—and don't forget to enjoy!

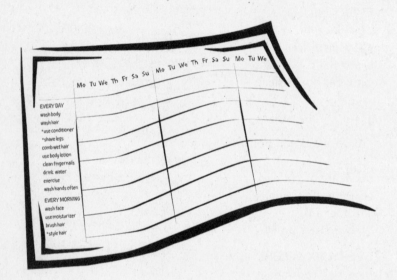

Some Cool Things About Having a Beauty Chart ...

_____

_____

_____

_____

_____

_____

_____

_____

_____

_____

_____

_____

_____

_____

_____

_____

_____

chapter six

Stylin'

I t was almost as if Betsy woke up one morning and all the clothes she had worn the week before were too small. Her mom announced that it was time for a shopping trip.

Hello-o! Every girl's dream!

At first, Betsy was thrilled. Lately, she'd been focusing more on what the other girls were wearing, and she knew exactly what she wanted — which, of course, was exactly what *they* had. She raced through the store, finding jeans like Madison's and tops like Taylor's and skirts like Ashleigh's. This was going to be sweet.

But when Betsy tried on the first outfit in the dressing room and stared at herself in the mirror, she watched her mouth turn down at the corners.

"It doesn't look like it does on Madison and Taylor and Ashleigh," Betsy said to her mom.

"Of course it doesn't," her mom said. "You have longer legs than Madison and you're curvier than Taylor. Besides, your hair is darker than all of theirs, so that isn't a good color for you."

Betsy stared hard into the mirror again. "I don't care," she said stubbornly. "I want to wear clothes like my friends!"

"I'm not buying you something that doesn't look right on you," her mom said — in that voice that meant "conversation over."

That's it, Betsy thought. *My life is ruined.*

GOT GOD?

If you read all the Scripture verses about clothes, you might think God can't make up his mind about what we're supposed to wear. Let's take them one at a time and see what God really has to say.

God does want you to look your best. The woman of noble character described in Proverbs "is clothed in fine linen and purple" (Proverbs 31:22). And not only that, but in her household, "all of them are clothed in scarlet" (verse 21).

That doesn't mean you have to wear the most expensive labels and always look like you just walked out of Limited Too. It means that when you put on clothes that look good and feel great on you, *that* says, "I want people to see the real me, a person who deserves respect."

"Best," in God's eyes, is different for everyone. And not only does God create you to be one of a kind, but he watches you with loving eyes, coaxing you to be who he made you to be. "[God] forms the hearts of all ... considers everything they do" (Psalm 33:15).

Does it make sense, then, that everybody should dress exactly the same? We totally understand about wanting the clothes "everybody" is wearing. Your grandmother probably *had* to have a poodle skirt, and your mom may have begged for acid-washed, pegged jeans. It's natural to want to feel like part of a group at this point in your life.

But it's also a time for learning what makes you unique, because, of course, you are. God is amazingly creative. Even identical twins have different personalities. Your own "specialness" is what you bring to your group of friends—what makes them love you. Your best look is clothes that match that.

God doesn't want you to get all freaked out about what you're going to wear. Jesus talked about that in his famous Sermon on the Mount.

"'And why do you worry about clothes? See how the lilies of the field grow. They do not labor or spin. Yet I tell you that not even Solomon in all his splendor was dressed like one of these. If that is how God clothes the grass of the field, which is here today and tomorrow is thrown into the fire, will he not much more clothe you, O you of little faith?'" —MATTHEW 6:28-30

He wasn't saying we can just step out of the shower and God will put clothes on us. He meant that clothes shouldn't be the most important thing on the entire planet for us. It's fun to have a trendy belt or the everybody-has-one poncho. It's also fun to play board games, stay up late giggling, and make valentines for the patients at the nursing home. It's all about balance. Look good and then get on with the other stuff.

God is way more interested in how we live than how we dress, because that's what truly makes us beautiful.

"Your beauty should not come from outward adornment... Instead, it should be that of your inner self, the unfading beauty of a gentle and quiet spirit, which is of great worth in God's sight." —1 PETER 3:3-4

This is kind of a no-brainer, but which of these choices do you think is more important to God:

What shoes I wear or how I treat my mom?
Whether I have a way-cool swimsuit or whether I'm nice to the school "outcasts"?
Which top I wear with which jeans, or what I say to my friend who's having a way bad day?

Duh-uh, huh?
So what does all of that mean for your wardrobe? Pick out clothes that

✦ help you feel like you're part of the group;
✦ allow you to be your unique self;
✦ aren't the center of your universe; and
✦ allow your natural, inner beauty to shine through.

How in the *world* are you going to do all that at the same time? Fortunately God doesn't ask us to do the impossible, so let's find out!

That Is SO Me

Have you ever felt like you were wearing somebody else's clothes? That's probably because what you had on didn't tell who you were. The first step is to find your personal style.
Circle one item in each list that comes closest to something you like to do.

(a) play softball   (b) play Scrabble   (c) play a pretend game

(a) have a pillow fight   (b) do a magazine quiz   (c) giggle and talk with friends

(a) ride my bike   (b) read a book   (c) dream up a story

(a) play a computer game   (b) check out a website   (c) IM a friend

(a) try snow boarding   (b) build the perfect snowman   (c) make snow angels

Count up your a's, b's, and c's.

_____ a's

_____ b's

_____ c's

If you had more a's than other letters, you may prefer the sporty casual style. Who can do all the moving around you like to do in dresses and frills and pointy-toed shoes? Go with clothes that are comfortable and fun, even when you have to get dressed up. You can never tell when somebody might want to race you, or there's a tree that has to be climbed...

If you had more b's than other letters, using your mind makes you happy. You might really like a classic, tailored style. Not dull, of course, but crisp lines and cool jackets and pants and skirts you can mix 'n' match. Smart clothes!

If you had more c's than other letters, you like to laugh big and cry hard. Yours is more than likely an all-girl romantic style. It's fashion that fits your dreamy self—maybe embroidery on your jeans, spangles on your purse, beads on your flip-flops. And of course, loads of pink.

If you had an almost-equal number of each letter, you are a girl of many moods. Probably your style is creative. You like to be a tomboy one day and a girly-girl the next—and keep everybody guessing. Go ahead and combine more than one style at a time. You know— clunky boots with a long, flowy skirt, or a baseball cap with sequins on it.

Write your style here _____

Here's the Deal

Being sporty, or tailored, or romantic, or creative doesn't mean you have to dress like that all the time. Maybe this time next year you'll change styles completely as you find out more about who you are. But since most of us don't have unlimited funds to spend on our wardrobes, it's best to make sure most of your clothes are the usual you.

Here are some suggestions to help you shop, either at the store or in your own closet.

Pants

Sporty — your favorite style jeans, fun sweats, cargo pants, easy-to-move-in shorts, slacks in great colors for dressing up

Tailored — crisp jeans, your favorite style khakis, sweats that have matching jackets, shorts with belts 'n' pockets, slacks that look fabulous with boots or slip-on flats

Romantic — jeans with pretty details such as embroidery, pastel sweats in soft fabrics like fleece, skorts, wrap-around pants

Creative — funky jeans like the cropped off kind with beaded patterns, yoga pants, safari shorts, gauchos

Tops

Sporty — long- and short-sleeved straight T-shirts, zippered hoodies, tank tops, blouses that don't have to be tucked in for dressing up

Tailored — long- and short-sleeved fitted T-shirts, turtleneck and crewneck sweaters, fresh-looking sleeveless blouses, fitted blouses with details such as tucks and pleats for dress up

Romantic — long- and short-sleeved T-shirts with girly details, fancy sweaters with faux fur or crocheted collars, peasant blouses, empire-waist tops for dress up

Creative — long- and short-sleeved T-shirts with unusual designs on them, bulky knit sweaters and ponchos, tanks tops that look like two, tunic tops with fun details for dress up

Skirts and Dresses

Sporty — khaki and denim A-line skirts, skorts, simple dresses in fabrics that breathe (like 100% cotton)

Tailored — straight and pleated skirts; long skirts with simple lines; dresses with belts, pockets, and collars

Romantic — skirts that swirl when you twirl; gathered skirts; dresses with sashes, pretty sleeves, and details at the hem

Creative — skirts with unexpected features like shiny beads on denim or oversized pockets; wrap-around skirts; dresses that look like they might have come from another country

Jackets or Coats (depending on where you live)

Sporty — jean jackets, down jackets, parkas, sweater-jackets

Tailored — blazers, peacoats, fitted ski jackets, long coats with simple lines

Romantic — short (to the waist) jackets, furry jackets and coats, pastel ponchos

Creative — funky jean jackets, colorful ponchos, bomber jackets, capes and shawls

That Is SO Me

Have you ever *really* wanted something everybody was wearing, and when you tried it on it pulled in weird places? Or made you look, well, funny?

That's because there are different **body shapes**, and not every piece of clothing looks good on every one of them. Keeping in mind that God created—and loves—all shapes and sizes of people, have some fun finding out what yours is right now.

Decide which one of these is closest to what you see when you look in a full-length mirror, wearing either your undies or clothes that fit pretty snugly.

Medium to tall and willowy, like a beautiful birch tree.
+ long and lean   + straight up and down

Short and pixie-like, like you could be a real-life Tinkerbell.
+ tiny features   + small and slim

Medium to tall and strong, like a one-woman powerhouse.
+ some muscle definition   + athletic build
+ a few curves here and there

Short and sturdy, like an undercover superhero.
+ some muscle definition   + a few curves, but not many
+ power in a small package   + athletic-looking

Medium to tall and curvy, like a little woman is about to burst through.
+ a real waist, and starting to develop breasts
+ kind of like an hourglass

Short and cuddly, like a favorite teddy bear.
+ soft and round   + curves all over
+ may be starting to develop breasts

The good new is there are clothes for every body type. The bad news is ... well, there is no bad news!

You get to choose:

_____ Do you want to show your body type just as it is?

_____ Do you want to coax it to look even more beautiful?

There is no right or wrong answer to that question. It's totally up to you, as long as you like what you see when you get dressed and look in the mirror. Remember that God wants us to do our very best with what he's given us.

To play up your long, lean form — Think long and straight; don't choose belts at your waist or fabrics with big designs all over; things that flow are perfect for you.

To look taller than you are — Wear the same color from top to bottom or pick stripes and patterns that go up and down; shoes with just a little bit of a heel are smashing on you.

To play up how tiny you are — Keep your skirts above your knees (with Mom's approval); your tops can come to your waist; cropped pants, capris, and skorts are precious on you.

> Since you'll be growing and changing shape a lot in these years, your body type will also probably change. Even though we suggest ways to tone down body features you aren't crazy about, try not to get freaked out about a rounded tummy or the fact that you're the tallest one in the class. Your body is becoming itself, and that is beautiful.

When you shop, buy clothes that fit you. You should never look like you've been stuffed into your outfit, no matter what the current style is. Be sure you can move around freely. Forget that your best friend wears two sizes smaller than you do. She's her size, you are yours. This is a free and exciting time in your life, so be comfy enough to have a blast!

To look shorter than you are — Keep your skirts at or below your knees; wear things that "cut you in half," like a different color on top than on the bottom or a belt at your waist; you were made for fabulous flats.

To put the focus on your strong, sturdy body — Wear clothes that cling a little, the way T-shirts and stretchy shirts do; stand-up collars and straight-leg pants are right for you; your body screams for classy athletic-looking clothes, but they don't have to be boyish.

To soften your sturdiness a little — Wear clothes that are fitted (but not tight) instead of boxy; go for a small touch of girly detail, like some embroidery on a jeans pocket or a hint of lace on a blouse; sleeves with a little bit of puff and round necklines were created just for you.

To enjoy your curves or fluffiness — Go for loose-fitting things like full blouses and wide-legged pants; pull on a bright poncho or a peasant skirt; anything really feminine will bring out your rosy girlishness.

To appear more streamlined — Wear things that just fit — not too tight, not too loose; choose tops, dresses, and jackets that curve in at the waist; you're the cutest thing on the planet in fun collars and interesting sleeves.

That Is SO Me

One of the most fun things about clothes is that they come in so many different colors. Since *we* come in so many different colors too, that's a good thing! It's amazing how the shades you were born to wear can make your natural beauty shine. Want to find your color code?

Take a good long look in a mirror in good light — and maybe ask your mom or another grown-up to consult with you. Then circle one description in each column that is *most* like you. (We haven't covered all the possibilities.)

Hair

red

blonde

dark

Skin

light

dark

Check your combination:

_____ red hair/light skin

_____ blonde hair/light skin

_____ blonde hair/dark skin

_____ dark hair/light skin

_____ dark hair/dark skin

Here's the Deal

Of course, wear any color you want that makes you happy. God created a whole rainbow of hues for us to enjoy. If you really want to bring out the beauty of your natural coloring, here are some suggestions. Get ready to dazzle yourself!

	Best Colors	Not So Wonderful
Red hair/ light skin	any shade of green or blue, warm red, soft gold	white, yellow, very pastel colors
Blonde hair/ light skin	pink, light blue, light green, red, green, violet, coral	black, yellow, very pastel colors
Blonde hair/ dark skin	white, pink, lavender, light green, purple	orange, fluorescent colors
Dark hair/ light skin	red, maroon, deep pink	beige, very pastel colors, orange
Dark hair/ dark skin	rich red, black, brown, purple, emerald green, bright blue, red	yellow, fluorescent colors

You can't go wrong if you match your clothes to the color of your eyes.

Color can have an influence on your mood and on the way people see you. How cool is that?

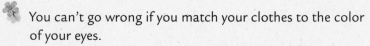

❖ Need a little energy or a confidence boost? Wear **red** — good for sports and times when you have to liven things up

* Need to feel like you have it together? **White** is your
  best bet—great for giving a speech in class, or playing
  in a piano recital.
* Need to state your independence? Put on your **green**.
  It's the perfect color for dealing with people who
  don't accept your "one-of-a-kind-ness."
* Need some calm? Clothe yourself in **light blue**—
  perfect for babysitting or when you're feeling jumpy.
* Need to be taken seriously? Get into your **dark blue**.
  Wear it if you're running for a class election or are
  determined to get that A in math.
* Need to be a little mysterious? **Black** is your answer.
  Since it's dramatic, it's just right for play tryouts, or
  anytime you want to keep them guessing.
* Need a hug or really want someone to trust you?
  Wear **pastels** (light shades of soft color). They're
  the thing on days when you feel lonely or especially
  loveable.

The absolutely most fun thing about putting an outfit together
is adding the accessories:

> hats
> scarves
> jewelry
> belts
> purses
> socks, tights
> shoes

Accessories are the magic in your wardrobe. They can

* turn a few basic items of clothing into a whole bunch of
  different outfits;
* draw attention to your best features;

❖ draw the focus away from things you're self-conscious about; and

❖ let you express your unique self in some major-fun ways.

There are certain things that draw attention wherever you put them:

❖ bright, warm colors like yellow, red, orange, and gold
❖ big designs
❖ sparkly, shiny things
❖ girly details

It's so simple to use accessories to pull someone's eye where you want it. Wear these attention getters near your best features:

Do you have great hair? Bring out the barrettes, the hair clips, and the funky scarves.
Have a tiny waist? Put on those belts, baby.
Really well-toned arms? Play them up with fun bracelets.
Nice neck? Necklaces were made for you.
Lovely legs? Go for the unique shoes, the perfect socks.

Write your own best features here:

~~~~~~

~~~~~~

~~~~~~

Use your imagination for ways to accessorize (use accessories) that will spotlight those physical gifts God gave you. Write your ideas here:

~~~~~~

~~~~~~

~~~~~~

If you have a physical feature you feel kind of funky about, keep the attention-getters away from there (but keep learning to accept that the way you were made is perfect in God's eyes):

Self-conscious about your ears? Not the best place for flashy jewelry, right?

Feeling like your hips are huge? (They probably aren't!) Don't hang a belt or scarf around them.

Always want to hide your fingernails? Stay away from rings (unless you've read chapter four).

And don't forget to show your true self when you're using accessories. Going back to your personal style, think about what is YOU. Here are some suggestions, but your own imagination is your best guide.

Sporty — ball caps, visors, pendants of your favorite sports teams, canvas shoulder bags, fun backpacks, the most perfect socks you can find, tennis shoes with personality

No matter what clothes and accessories you decide to wear, ask yourself, Does God want to see me in this? Does he want me showing a lot of skin that's better kept private? Is he going to be happy with some disrespectful saying on my T-shirt? Does he want me decked out in an outfit that makes me look way older than I am? When your mom says you can't wear your jeans that low or your top that high, she's guiding you by these questions. Try asking the questions yourself before she has to say, "You are SO not going anywhere dressed like that!"

Tailored — sleek hats, wool scarves, gloves, simple jewelry, purses to match your shoes, touches of fun in belts and buttons and socks

Romantic — sun hats, fuzzy winter caps with matching scarves and gloves, dainty jewelry (wherever you can hang it!), bows, lace, sparkly purses

Creative — berets, newsboy caps, chunky jewelry, belts and scarves galore — worn in unexpected places — funky purses, colored shoes

Although decisions about what clothes are bought for you are up to the grown-ups in your family, you can keep those decisions from turning into battles by following some of these tips. Someday you'll be using your own money for your wardrobe, so these are good **shopping skills** to learn for the future too.

- Know how much money there is to spend and don't try to persuade your folks to go outside their budget. You can pretty much tell what the finances are at your house, so why try to wheedle an expensive pair of jeans out of your mom when you know things are tight? If this is hard for you, try earning some money to buy a few things yourself. When you have to fork over your own cash for that new have-to-have-it, you might find out you really *don't* have to have it after all.

- Ask your parents what things they will absolutely not allow you to wear, and then don't even go to those racks in the store. They'll be impressed with how mature you are.

- Look for things that will go with what you already have. You might want new colors too, but be sure to choose things that will mix and match.

To really save money, watch for sales. Many stores have sales right after Christmas and right before school starts. Some stores have promotions, like a reward for bringing in a good report card or a coupon in the newspaper or mail. Remember that just because it's on sale doesn't mean you'll save money; be sure you're actually going to wear it.

If you're dying for something trendy, suggest to your parents that you buy it at one of the less expensive stores. That way if you only wear it until it goes out of style (like maybe **next month**), it won't be a huge waste of money.

Remember that it's better to have a few perfect-for-you, good quality pieces of clothing than a whole closet full of stuff that really isn't your best look. Don't forget that you can create different outfits with fun accessories. And besides, what rule says you have to wear something different every single day? If it's great on you this Tuesday, it will still look fabulous next Tuesday!

If there is no shopping trip planned for the near future, try "shopping" in your own closet and drawers.

Put all your clothes in two piles:
- things that don't fit you or have never been and will never be you. Ask if you can give them to charity (or your little sister!)

❀ things that fit and have possibilities for your style, body type, and coloring

🐞 Pick up each item in the I'm-keeping-it pile. Before you put it back in the closet or into a drawer, make a plan for it.

❀ See how many other things it goes with.

❀ Have fun putting surprising colors next to each other; use accessories to bring colors together. (Purple pants will go with a yellow top if you have a yellow and purple bracelet to tie them in.)

❀ If it isn't exactly your style, see what you can put with it to capture the real you. (You may not be into that romantic pink skirt, but put on a jean jacket and some clean tennies — and you're your sporty self.)

🐞 If you really love putting outfits together, write the combinations you discover on separate cards and pick one when it's time to get dressed. (You can even put different types of outfits on different color cards — pink for dressing up, yellow for school . . .) If you would rather have your tonsils out than do that, just put like things together so it's easy for you to grab an outfit and go.

You're Good to Go

Whether you're jazzed about clothes, or your mom has to drag you out to shop, or you're somewhere in between, it's good to find the best wardrobe that

✦ helps you feel like you're part of the group;
✦ allows you to be your unique self;
✦ isn't the center of your universe; and
✦ allows your natural, inner beauty to shine through.

Everybody needs that! So try this "dream wardrobe" activity to head you in the right direction. (This is fun to do with a friend.)

Step 1: Gather some magazines and catalogs picturing girls your age. Or, if you're artistic, get out some paper and your drawing materials.

Step 2: Pull out or draw pictures of clothes that

* suit your style (sporty, tailored, romantic, creative);
* are right for your body shape (medium to tall and willowy, short and pixie-like, medium to tall and strong, short and sturdy, medium to tall and curvy, short and cuddly);
* bring out your natural coloring (red hair/light skin, blonde hair/light skin, blonde hair/dark skin, dark hair/light skin, dark hair/dark skin); and
* are things you need for your life (school clothes, dress-up clothes, play clothes, clothes for your special activities).

Step 3: Arrange your pictures however you want to. We suggest one of these display ideas:

* a scrapbook
* a collage
* a box of colored folders
* a bulletin board

Step 4: Look at your "dream wardrobe" every now and then and realize how uniquely beautiful you are. God really likes it when you do that.

When I Loook at My Dream Wardrobe, I See a Girl Who Is ...

_____

_____

_____

_____

_____

_____

_____

_____

_____

_____

_____

_____

_____

_____

_____

_____

_____

_____

Don't You
HATE THAT?

B etsy slumped into the chair in the doctor's office and
blinked back tears.

   Just an hour ago she'd grinned at herself in the mirror
at home because not only did she look ... well, like her own self,
but she felt great. She had been planning to go shopping with her
mom right after her appointment at the eye doctor — maybe pick
up the new sandals she'd been saving her own money for. And
then they were going to the library so she could get a book about
kachina dolls, because she was totally fascinated with them, and
then ...

   But once again Betsy tried to keep from crying right out loud
in front of the doctor and her mom, who were discussing her
glasses.

   Glasses! Just when she was starting to like herself, now she
had to stick glasses on her face and look like an owl. She could
almost hear the comments at school: Jason saying, "Hey, Four
Eyes. Bet you think you're like this genius now." The mean girls
saying, "Ugh. Why didn't you get contacts?" Her own friends
saying, "They don't look that bad, Bets. Really. You're still
pretty." *Right*, Betsy thought miserably. *Pretty as a raccoon.*

   She slid further down in the chair. She didn't want to go to
the shoe store or the library anymore. She just wanted to go home
and hide her head under a pillow.

That Is SO Me

Here's a list of "Beauty Bummers" some girls say they'd rather live without. Get a pencil and look at each *bummer* on the list.

Put a check mark if you have that particular thing in your life. If you do, circle the best description of how it affects you.

___ *glasses*
   a. I hate them.
   b. They're okay.
   c. They're so me!
   d. What glasses?

___ *braces*
   a. I'm counting the days until I get them off.
   b. I don't mind them most of the time.
   c. It's cool to have braces.
   d. What's the big deal?

___ *being tall*
   a. I feel like a giraffe.
   b. It's not that bad.
   c. Are you kidding? Tall girls look so good in their clothes!
   d. Who cares?

___ *being big*
   a. It's so embarrassing to be huge.
   b. I don't know—I guess it's just the way I am.
   c. There's so much more of me to love!
   d. So what?

___ *scars, birthmarks, or moles*
   a. I wish I could just put a bag over my head.
   b. People who know me just get used to it.

c. I'm one of a kind!

d. I forgot about it until just now.

___ *other physical feature kids tease you about*
  a. I'm totally having plastic surgery when I turn eighteen.
  b. Whatever. They'll grow up someday.
  c. I inherited it and I'm proud of it!
  d. I don't even get why they tease me.

If you didn't have any check marks, read on anyway. Every girl has to deal with something she doesn't like about herself at some point. Besides, this chapter will show you how to help a girlfriend who might be struggling with a "beauty bummer" right now.

If you circled any a's, you're having a hard time, aren't you? People can be mean, and as we've said, "the world" in general can make you think you have to be perfect. As you read on for help, remember that you are already beautiful, and getting more so every day.

If you circled any b's, whatever some people consider a bummer doesn't really bother you that much. Wouldn't it be fun, though, to make it one of the best things about you? Read on!

If you circled any c's, you probably could have written this chapter yourself! You have the right idea. Keep reading so you can have even more fun with your unique look and encourage other girls to do the same. You can make a difference.

If you circled any d's, you don't even see any of this as a problem. Very cool. We would tell you not to even bother with this chapter, except that it will help you understand why other girls get upset. The last thing you want to do is tell a friend who's stressing about her braces to "just get over it." But if you read on, you can help her get over it—without losing her as a friend.

Here's the Deal

No matter what letters you circled in *That Is SO Me*, there are three things everyone needs to learn in life:

* How to know what you can change and what you can't
* How to change what can be changed, or at least make it a little better
* How to accept what can't be changed, and maybe even make it work for you

For example, let's say you have what you consider to be the longest nose in the galaxy, and other kids call you Pinocchio until you want to smack somebody. Consider the three questions.

Can I change it? Not unless you have plastic surgery, and that isn't even an option at your age. Besides, who knows — your face may grow into your nose and make you look fabulous.

How can I make it a little better? Wear your hair parted on the side and not too flat on top. Choose colors that bring out the color of your eyes.

How can I accept it and make it work for me? It's probably a family trait, so be proud of that. Instead of thinking of it as "honkin' huge," find another way to describe it. Is it noble? Strong? Comical? Queenly? Call it that in your mind and it will change everything, especially when somebody thinks he's original and calls you Pinocchio for the forty-fifth time.

Get the idea? Let's see what you can do with the Basic Beauty Bummers that will bring out more of that beautiful you.

Can I change it? Not unless you want to ruin your eyesight. There's nothing beautiful about squinting your eyes to see.

How can I make it a little better? Take your time picking out frames you like that look great on you. There's a shape and color and style for every person. Ask the folks at the optical store to help you find the perfect ones. Contact lenses are a choice, and they actually help you see better than glasses do. Just remember that they require a lot of care, are easy to lose, and sometimes hard to get used to. You might want to wait until you're older.

Glasses

How can I accept it and make it work for me? Think about having fewer headaches and getting better grades because you can actually see! Remember that glasses make a person look really smart. Make yours a part of your unique style, and people will say, "You look so much cuter with your glasses."

Can I change it? Probably not, especially if you really have some teeth and jaw issues that can affect your health (not to mention your looks).

How can I make it a little better? Did you know braces—and rubber bands—come in different colors as well as in clear and silver? How fun is that? You can't hide them, so why not let them sparkle? To get those braces off as fast as you can (the average time to wear them is two and a half years), brush, floss, and avoid super hard or sticky, gooey foods.

Braces

How can I accept it and make it work for me? Your teeth are going to be amazing when you get the braces off, and that will last for the rest of your life. And you certainly aren't alone. How many other girls in your grade are wearing them—and looking adorable? The best thing you can do is smile big and bright. You'll be unforgettable.

Can I change it? Not a chance.

How can I make it a little better? Remember the advice in chapter six about what to wear? You'll still be the same height, but you can look shorter.

How can I accept it and make it work for me? There are

almost no minuses in being tall and lots of pluses. You look wonderful in clothes. Women who are tall are often automatically respected and considered to be leaders by other people. In a very short time, you'll really grow into your height and feel less gangly and klutzy. Meanwhile, learn to play basketball and volleyball. Dream of being a model. Enjoy the view. And most of all, stand up straight and proud.

Can I change it? You can't change the fact that you have big, healthy bones and a strong frame. You can keep from being overweight, but you'll probably never be skinny. (You would look pretty funny with no meat on those wonderful bones!)

How can I make it a little better? Go back to chapter six and look at what clothes can soften your look a little. Be sure to eat good healthy stuff rather than junk and fast food. Get lots of fun exercise—at least five times a week.

How can I accept it and make it work for me? You're strong and robust. That's a great look! Go out for some sports. People seem to trust those who are bigger than they are, so let your friends have confidence in you. Be comfortable in your own skin. You can make a difference, because people will always notice you. Live large!

Can I change it? Sometimes you can. Usually removing or toning down these kinds of things involves a doctor. Talk honestly with your parents about how you feel.

How can I make it a little better? Trying to cover up things like birthmarks or moles usually only draws attention

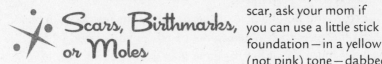
Scars, Birthmarks, or Moles

to them. If you have a scar, ask your mom if you can use a little stick foundation — in a yellow (not pink) tone — dabbed with powder.

How can I accept it and make it work for me? Think of it as a mark that gives your face character. Many models keep a mole as a trademark (and call it a beauty mark). A scar shows that you were strong enough to go through something painful. Focus on the other things that are beautiful about you. When people stare, ask if they have any questions. Remember that these things are the prints left by your life as you live it.

GOT GOD?

Even if you have the best attitude ever, there may still be kids and even adults who can't leave your glasses or your chicken pox scars or your rosy round cheeks alone. It's embarrassing. It's maddening. It's enough to make you point out *their* wart or buck teeth or bald head.

Before you hurl back an insult or run to the restroom in tears, try to remember this: When someone teases you about a "flaw," that says more about her (or him) than it does about you. A mouth full of braces or a face full of freckles tells nothing about you as a person. But a rude remark from a person's mouth announces that he or she is at that moment one of these:

* ✳ thoughtless
* ✳ careless
* ✳ insensitive
* ✳ jealous
* ✳ needing to feel better than you
* ✳ just plain mean

So what do you do about it? God says:

"Whoever corrects a mocker invites insult."
— PROVERBS 9:7

 Don't argue with a teaser or you'll just be teased more.

"A fool shows his annoyance at once, but a prudent man overlooks an insult."
— PROVERBS 12:16

 Ignore teasing. Don't even react in front of the teaser. (But it's okay to go away and cry if you need to.)

"Do not repay evil with evil or insult with insult, but with blessing."

— 1 PETER 3:9

Don't try to get back at the teaser with insults of your own. Be your own best self, and compliment her honestly, help her if she needs it, and refuse to talk trash about her behind her back.

"Love your enemies and pray for those who persecute you."

— MATTHEW 5:44

Ask God to heal whatever is causing people to tease you until it hurts. They may not change, but you will. It's hard to keep hating someone you're praying for.

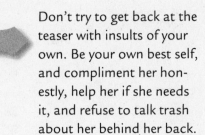

You're Good to Go

Get a BIG piece of paper (the kind that comes on a roll) and lie down on it. Have someone trace an outline of you. If you can't come up with large paper, sketch an outline of yourself on the biggest piece you can find.

Using markers, crayons, or pencils in fun colors, draw in all your features that you love or that you hardly even think about. Don't use any black. Make it as beautiful as you are.

Now, using black, draw in anything you're not happy about.

Look at the final picture. There's a whole lot more color than black, isn't there? Even if you have "flaws" they have *nothing* on all that is beautiful about you.

What did you discover when you created that picture of yourself?

When I Created That Picture of Myself I Discovered...

chapter eight

What
ABOUT ...?

When Betsy took off her jacket in science class, Madison squealed. Ashley gasped. Jason said, "Dude is that *real?*"

Betsy looked down at the fake butterfly tattoo she had put on her shoulder that morning. "Do *you* think it's real?" she asked.

Jason squinted his eyes at it. "Nah — that's totally bogus."

"Your parents would never let you get a tattoo!" Madison said, mouth hanging open in horror.

Jason grunted. "Too bad. I think it looks kinda cool."

Betsy felt her cheeks get warm, and she smiled secretly to herself. Nobody had ever said anything of hers was cool before.

Was that why people got real tattoos? she wondered.

Here's the Deal

You don't have to look very far to see somebody wearing The Bad Girl Look. You know the one:

- ❖ pierced nose, tongue, lip, eyebrow — you name it
- ❖ tattoos
- ❖ hair colors *nobody* was born with

- clothes that scream, "I don't care who you are — you aren't the boss of me."
- accessories that suggest violence or sexiness — for example, a necklace with a skull, a belt made of bullets, a belly button ring (proudly displayed)

Most of the time, you see The Bad Girl Look on teenagers and young adults. But these days it's showing up more and more on middle schoolers and even girls your age. What's up with that?

There are probably as many reasons for wanting to tattoo and pierce as there are people who do it. These are some of the main explanations behind decking out in all black or piercing every space on an ear:

'I want to be different.'

'It's my body, and I have a right to do whatever I please with it.'

'It's my way of expressing how sick I am of everybody telling me who to be.'

'I like to weird people out, especially adults who try to control me.'

'If people really want to know the real me, they have to get past the way I look. If they judge me by my appearance, I don't want to know them.'

'I want people to look at me.'

What's wrong with that? Haven't we been saying through this whole book that you should be your unique self? That you should dress in a way that shows who you are? That you shouldn't worry about what everybody else thinks?

You're right. We have. But take a close look at each of those reasons for going for The Bad Girl Look and see why they're very different from what we've been telling you.

"I want to be different." That's totally normal. But if all your friends or half the class are also dying their hair green and piercing their eyebrows, how does that make you different? It doesn't take much imagination to fit yourself into a "look."

"It's my body, and I have the right to do whatever I please with it."

- First of all, that right doesn't kick in until you're at least eighteen *and* supporting yourself. Not only that, but no piercing is legal without a parent being present until you're sixteen, and in some states until you're eighteen or even twenty-one. Even with a parent's permission, by law a tattoo can't be done until you're eighteen. Going to someone who is willing to ignore the rules and give you a piercing or a tattoo anyway is dangerous. You can be sure he or she will ignore the safety and cleanliness rules too.

- If the piercer's instruments and hands aren't totally clean, you can get an infection. That is SO not fun, especially inside your nose or mouth.

- A tattoo involves someone injecting permanent dye under your skin. (Ouch!) If the needle isn't completely germ-free, you can get hepatitis, even AIDS. It just isn't worth the risk.

- Even if you went to the cleanest place on the planet, there are other risks with piercing:
  - It's easy to swallow a tongue ring or stud.
  - A belly button piercing can get infected just from getting caught on your jeans or the buttons on your shirt.

- If rings get torn out, it can be painful (and bloody ... EW!).
- An allergic reaction can leave a permanent ring like a tattoo on your skin.
- An infection in the hard part of your ear (not the lobe) can result in your ear losing its shape and becoming deformed.

Besides all that, who does your body really belong to? We'll talk about that more in the pages ahead.

"It's my way of expressing how sick I am of everybody telling me who to be." It's actually healthy to want to be your unique self. The trick is to truly know *you* and express *that*, not your feelings. Is *bad* who you really are? Is *angry*? You might feel like nobody gets you, but there are a whole lot of healthier and safer and less permanent ways to deal with that feeling. We'll talk about those later in this chapter.

If you do get permission to pierce your ears, it would be neat to think of it as God's ancient people did. A servant who pledged lifelong service to his beloved master had his ear pierced as a sign of devotion. Since your master is God, how cool! Be sure to go to a place approved by the Association of Professional Piercers, and keep the holes infection-free by cleaning them and your earrings with hydrogen peroxide or the stuff the store may give you.

"I like to weird people out, especially adults who try to control me." And you probably will! But what is the result? Ever noticed the way teachers watch the "bad kids"? They're always on them, ready to pounce. Teachers and other adults don't give second chances to kids who do things just to gross them out. Sometimes the rebels get in trouble for things they don't even do, just because they look like the type who would. Life's tough enough without inviting trouble.

"If people really want to know the real me, they have to get past the way I look. If they judge me by my appearance, I don't want to know them." What is that about? The whole point of looking like you is so people will see a real person and want to get to know you better. If you make people work that hard to see who you are inside, you waste a lot of time that could be spent sharing great friendships. Like it or not, when someone sees a girl who looks mean or tough or disrespectful, that person is going to assume she is, even if she isn't.

"I want people to look at me." We all want attention, and that isn't always a bad thing. If no one pays attention to you, you won't have friends, you won't be able to share what an awesome person you are, and you'll be pretty lonely. But you need the right *kind* of attention.

❖ The right kind of attention sounds like, "You're special." "I've never known anyone like you." "I like being around you because you don't try to be something you're not." You are communicating, "Feel free to look around all you want and let me know if I can help you."

❖ The wrong kind of attention sounds like, "Dude, what are you trying to prove?" "I'm not inviting you to my party. You don't look like very nice." "I'm scared of you."

✜ Do you want to communicate, "If you aren't going to buy anything, I suggest you leave the store"?

It's hard if you don't get positive attention at home, and that can make you think that any kind of notice is better than none. But that isn't true. Just ahead, we'll talk about shining as the real you instead of making up somebody to be. First, let's see what might be pushing you to go to extremes, even in the secret places in your mind.

That Is SO Me

Put a star (*) next to each paragraph that describes you at least some of the time. If the description doesn't sound like you at all, leave it blank.

_____ A

I have to say, "Mom?" or "Dad!" like forever, before they answer me. It seems like my parents praise my brother (or sister) way more than they praise me. When I do things right, it's like no big deal, but if I mess something up, you would think I committed a crime. I don't think I'm good at anything—at least nobody says I am.

_____ B

Sometimes I feel like my own family doesn't get me. People say things like, "You sure aren't like your sister (or your mom or anybody else in the whole family)." Kids at school look at me like I'm weird. My parents are always trying to get me to be less this or more that (like less shy and more athletic). It doesn't really bother me that I'm kinda different, but it obviously bothers a lot of other people.

_____ C

I always have to keep my bedroom door open. If I just want to hang out by myself, people ask me what's wrong or try to make me "join in." I get in trouble for arguing, and when I want to do something new, I hear stuff like, "You're not old enough yet." There are things I want to decide for myself, but I'm not allowed to—things like how I wear my hair or what activities I do after school.

Here's the Deal

If you put a star next to any of the descriptions in *That Is SO Me*, you might have one of these feelings:

angry
frustrated
hurt
resentful
afraid
just constantly cranky

Even if things aren't really as bad as you think they are (since most parents are doing a pretty good job), the way you see them can still make you want to punch a pillow, bite your brother, or scream at whoever happens to be standing nearby. And sometimes those thoughts and feelings can make you want to dress like a Bad Girl, wear a big ol' stud in your lip, and dye your hair some impossible color. At the very least they can push you to hate every outfit or hairstyle your mom suggests — just because.

The thing is, lashing out at people or dressing up like a hoochie mama doesn't change those feelings. It can even make them worse, because people are going to get so focused on the way you look, they aren't going to discover how bad you feel so they can help you.

Why do something that doesn't work? Let's find out what *does*.

If you starred A on That Is SO Me, it sounds like you need *attention* — the kind that makes you smile and glow. The kind that nudges you to be *more* helpful, brave, friendly or whatever it was that got people to notice you in the first place. That doesn't mean stand on a table in the cafeteria and yell, "Look at what I did!" It does mean the following:

✿ Do the things you do well because you enjoy them, not so everybody will say, "Wow."

✿ Discover what it is about you that even one person seems to like, and go with it—whether it's the way you smile, how well you listen, or the fact that you never spread gossip.

✿ Give *other* people the kind of attention *you* want—praise, sympathy, a big laugh at their jokes.

✿ If you're feeling a little neglected by one of your parents, rather than whine or accuse, ask for some time together—even just an hour alone.

✿ If you don't think you do anything well, try things that sound fun or interesting to you. Have such a blast doing them that you don't worry about anyone noticing how good you are at them (although people probably will).

✿ Remember that God is always watching you enjoy your successes, being there the instant you need him. You have *his* undivided attention.

If you starred B on That Is SO Me, it may be that you're struggling to be *accepted for who you really are* — or you're trying to *find out* who you are. That doesn't mean that whatever you do, you think everybody should say, "That's just the way she is." It means you want that calm feeling that comes when you don't have to worry whether people think you're lame or geeky or just generally strange. Try some of these:

❖ Don't hang out with people who make fun of you. Don't even try to be friends with them.

❖ Find at least one person who appreciates your special qualities or interests—your book collection, your huge vocabulary, your total love of cats. Invite her over or ask her to sit with you at lunch.

❖ Show your family or your classmates that the very thing they want to change in you can really be a good thing for *them.* If they say you're too quiet, listen when they have a problem. If they say you're not athletic, cheer from the sidelines when they're playing, or make a banner, or write encouraging notes if they lose. The people who love you will begin to appreciate who you are instead of trying to turn you into what they think would make you happier.

❖ Love who you are. Nobody is more appealing than a for-real person.

❖ Remember that God made your true self. He's there to help you be just that.

If you starred C on That Is SO Me, it just may be that you *want to be allowed to grow up.* Perhaps the adults in your life don't see that, or they think you're trying to be older too fast. It's sort of like walking around in shoes that are too small for you and are pinching your toes.

That doesn't mean you should ignore the limits grown-ups put on you, because you need some. But if you feel you're being treated like a baby, you can try some of these:

✳ Be mature in ways that are right for your age — doing chores without having to be reminded and not slacking off in school.

✳ Be mature in ways that will surprise people — offering to watch your little brother so your mom can take a bubble bath, refusing to exclude a girl everyone else is leaving out, putting part of your allowance in the collection plate.

✳ Make a list of things you know are not your decision — like what time you go to bed or whether you go to school. Then make a list of things you would like to decide about your life, within your parents' limits, of course — such as how you wear your hair, what books you read for fun, what sports you play. Show both lists to your parents and ask if you can make at least one of the choices on the second list.

* If you need more privacy, ask for it politely. "May I have my door closed for an hour after school?" "Could you please knock before you come in the bathroom?"
* Take care of your stuff. Keep your room at least a little bit organized. Be "together" when it's time to leave for school. Those things show that you *are* growing up.
* Dream about how you want your life to be when you're in charge of it. Keep a journal or make a scrapbook about your imagined future.
* With your friends, or alone, pretend you're grown-up. You're never too old for dress up or acting games.
* Look forward to things to come—going to high school football games, getting a driver's license, wearing make-up, going shopping with your girlfriends, playing on a school team. But don't hurry them. Enjoy what you have right now—no money worries, time to play and daydream, permission to giggle your head off.

> Be careful not to judge other people who have a lot of piercings or tattoos or disturbing jewelry. Now you know that many kids who go for that look have things they're trying to deal with. Pray that they'll let God help them, and in the meantime, don't just decide that they're "bad."

* Pray—a lot—for God to help you grow up just at the rate he wants you to.
* Remember that you can't rush God.

Notice that none of the suggestions above have anything to do with

+ shocking people with your hairdo,
+ grossing people out with your piercings,
+ making a statement with your tattoo,
+ going to extremes with your clothes so people will notice you, or
+ showing zero respect for yourself because it feels like nobody else respects you.

Most of the suggestions we've made are positive things—do's, not don'ts. But it can be hard to do positive things when negative actions seem easier. That, of course, is why God is there for you.

But if you're angry or frustrated and think a tattoo or a nose ring will make you feel better, some of God's other words are much more helpful. They describe a Father who totally gets it and will guide you *through* your feelings and help you *solve* your problems in healthier actually ways that are much for you, and that work.

> "Do you not know that your body is a temple of the Holy Spirit, who is in you, whom you have received from God? ... Therefore honor God with your body."
> —1 CORINTHIANS 6:19-20

Step One — Find a private place and vent to God — out loud or in a journal — about what you're feeling.

> "Trust in him at all times, O people;
>   pour out your hearts to him,
> for God is our refuge."   —PSALM 62:8

Step Two — Ask God for what you need: help sorting it out, courage to talk to your parents, strength to be yourself ...

> "In the morning, O LORD, you hear my voice;
>   in the morning I lay my requests before you."
>   —PSALM 5:3

Step Three — Wait and listen for God's answer. Keep talking to God and you'll know what to do.

> "Wait for the LORD;
>   be strong and take heart
> and wait for the LORD." — PSALM 27:14

Step Four — Do what God tells you, whether his instructions come to you through the Bible; a wise grown-up; or a still, small voice inside.

> "Give me understanding, and I will keep your law
>   and obey it with all my heart." — PSALM 119:34

Step Five — Repeat Steps One through Four, every day. The things that make you think you want The Bad Girl Look will be healed, and you will be more beautiful than ever.

> "God is our refuge and strength,
>   an ever-present help in trouble." — PSALM 46:1

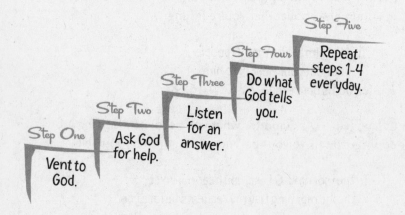

Step One — Vent to God.

Step Two — Ask God for help.

Step Three — Listen for an answer.

Step Four — Do what God tells you.

Step Five — Repeat steps 1-4 everyday.

You're Good to Go

Whether you have big issues or just occasionally get annoyed about a particular thing, it's healing to express how you feel in ways that don't hurt you or anyone else.

Start by writing down one thing that makes you feel angry, frustrated, resentful, hurt, or just plain cranky. Then choose one of these healthy ways to get your feelings out there where you can see them.

Write fast and furiously in a private journal until you think you've said it all about that issue. Go back to it whenever you get those feelings and write some more.

Paint a picture that shouts what you're feeling. Nobody else has to be able to tell what it is — just you. Finger painting is the most satisfying, but brush painting works too.

Make a clay figure that's just like what's going on inside you. Feel free to turn it back into a ball and make a new figure whenever you want to.

You'll be amazed at how much better you'll feel and at the things that come into your head while you're writing, sculpting, or painting. Being creative with your hands frees your mind up so you can solve your problems. That's totally better than trying to look like The Bad Girl.

When I Did My "You're Good to Go" Project I Felt...

chapter nine

Inside
OUT

Although all the other kids were crowded around the classroom bulletin board, Betsy didn't want to see the list her teacher, Mrs. Post, was putting up. She hadn't liked the idea of voting for "class favorites" from the start, and then when the class had decided on the categories, she'd liked it even less.

Cutest Girl, Cutest Boy
Smartest Girl, Smartest Boy
Most Talented Girl, Most Talented Boy
Best Dressed Girl, Best Dressed Boy
Most Athletic Girl, Most Athletic Boy
Most Popular Girl, Most Popular Boy
Funniest Girl, Funniest Boy

When Mrs. Post had asked if there were any more suggestions, Betsy raised her hand. She was getting better about that. "How about Most Honest?" Betsy said.

One of the girls — who was sure to be voted Most Popular — snorted. "That's lame," she said.

"No negative responses," Mrs. Post said. "All suggestions will be considered."

Jason grunted. "What about Most Ridiculous, then?"

What about Most Rude? Betsy thought.

Mrs. Post considered Jason's suggestion for about three seconds, but she wrote Betsy's on the board. Then Madison raised her hand.

"Friendliest," she said.

"Isn't that the same as Most Popular?" somebody said.

"It *should* be," Mrs. Post said. She frowned. "But it isn't always. Let's make that a separate category."

There was a lot of eye rolling.

But everyone had voted. And now as Mrs. Post parted the crowd to step away from the bulletin board, they all rushed the list, pushing and elbowing to be the first to know who the favorites were.

Everyone but Betsy. She sat in her desk, and she thought.

She had filled her beauty chart with stickers every day for months. She'd cleaned out her closet, and gone shopping with her mom, and felt real (and cute!) in her clothes. She had a new haircut and the most fun glasses ever, and only one person had teased her about them. She was praying for Jason every night.

Just when I was feeling like I might be beautiful just being me, Betsy thought, *they have to go and have a contest. I know who's going to get Cutest Girl and Best Dressed, and then everybody's going to think they have to totally look like them.*

Why did we have to choose "favorites"?

"Hey, Betsy!" Madison called from the bulletin board. "Guess which one you got!"

"Me?" Betsy said.

Now what?

Let's leave Betsy in suspense while we look at one more beauty ingredient — the most important one. After you've read this chapter, you'll have a chance to write the ending for Betsy, in *"That's What I'm Talkin' About."* Yours will be the final vote!

Here's the Deal

In this book, we've talked about

- ❖ you being your unique self;
- ❖ hair care;
- ❖ face facts;
- ❖ mani's and pedi's;
- ❖ getting smooth;
- ❖ fashion fun;
- ❖ The Bad Girl Look; and
- ❖ beauty bummers.

At the same time, we've hinted that who you are inside—your true, genuine, authentic self—is really what makes you a good lookin' gal. Now let's put the spotlight on that. If you don't remember another thing from this book (although hopefully that's not the case), remember this:

No matter how great a girl's hair, skin, nails, and clothes are—no matter how free she is of physical "flaws"—she will not be truly beautiful unless she shines from within.

She may win beauty contests or get a modeling contract or have boys flocking all around her. That means she's cute, or pretty, or practically perfect from head to toe. That doesn't mean she's beautiful.

A beautiful girl can have bad hair days, pimples, and hairy legs. She may not be able to sit still long enough to have a manicure or tweeze her eyebrows or worry that she towers over the whole rest of her class. She is beautiful because she focuses on these beauty secrets:

- ✦ confidence in her God-given gifts and talents that smoothes her brow
- ✦ joy that makes her eyes sparkle; honesty that makes them clear

- a sense of fun that gives her a dazzling smile
- energy in helping, sharing, and doing her best that makes her skin glow; kindness that softens it
- positive, encouraging words that make her lips lovely
- love for God, others, and herself that makes her attractive in a way no one can explain

That Is SO Me

Try an experiment so you'll see exactly what we mean.

Pick out a few girls you know who are considered cute or pretty. Watch them whenever you can. If you see one being rude to someone or using bad language, watch even more closely. Is she still pretty? What if someone caught her on camera at that moment? Would a magazine put it on the cover? (Don't point this out to the girl. Go back to chapter eight and review what to do.)

Go through a magazine you can tear pages out of. Collect all the pictures of what you think are pretty girls. Then put them in two piles: (1) girls who you'd like to be friends with, and (2) girls you might steer clear of. What's the difference? Which pile shows truly beautiful girls (from what you can tell)?

Make a list of the people you love. Next to each one, write in a few words why you love that person so much. Then picture each one in your mind or look at the person for real if you can. Do you see any of those people as ugly? If you want to watch someone become even more beautiful, tell the person why you love him or her. You'll be more beautiful too.

Wouldn't it be cool if you could just say, "From now on, I am going to be confident, joyful, fun-loving, energized, kind, encouraging, and loving"? It would be like an instant beauty treatment.

Developing those qualities takes time—and it takes God. We can't do it by reading books or following rules or copying women we admire—although those things help. We can only do it by turning our whole selves to God, every day, so he can remind us, heal us, forgive us, and lead us. Now that *is* a great beauty treatment, and there's enough to last a whole lifetime.

> "'Love the Lord your God with all your heart and with all your soul and with all you mind.' This is the first and greatest commandment. And the second is like it: 'Love your neighbor as yourself.'"
> — MATTHEW 22:37-39

These are the inner beauty basics God gives us. Do these things every day, just the way you do the things on your beauty chart. This is your beauty manual.

> "Whatever is true, whatever is noble, whatever is right, whatever is pure, whatever if lovely, whatever is admirable — if anything is excellent or praiseworthy — think about such things.... put it into practice. And the God of peace will be with you."
> — PHILIPPIANS 4:8-9

> "Live in harmony with one another; be sympathetic, love as brothers, be compassionate and humble. Do not repay evil with evil or insult with insult, but with blessing."
> — 1 PETER 3:8-9

Learn these verses if you want to, but definitely live by them. If you do, you will be one gorgeous little woman.

You're Good to Go

We usually think of being sympathetic and compassionate and humble as things we do for other people. But it's just as important to apply them to ourselves. Jesus said, "Love your neighbor *as yourself.*" If we don't know how to treat ourselves lovingly, how will we be able to care about other people that way?

So let's start the inner-beauty treatment with you. Next to each beautiful quality God wants you to have, write down one thing you could do for yourself to show yourself that lovely trait. The prompts are there to help you, but you can also come up with your own if you like.

Be sympathetic with yourself.
(For example: Let yourself cry about _____.
Rock yourself to sleep.)

_____

_____

Be compassionate to yourself.
(For example: Stop beating yourself up about _____.
Hug yourself.)

_____

_____

Be humble about yourself.
(For example: Give God the credit for _____.
Write God a thank you note.)

_____

_____

Repay yourself for a mistake with blessing.
(For example: Forgive yourself for _____.
Take a cleansing bath.)

_____

_____

Be honest with yourself.
(For example: Admit that you _____.
Apologize to yourself.)

Stand up for yourself.
(For example: Go to _____ (person who has
hurt you) and explain (lovingly) how he/she has hurt you.
Share a cookie.)

That's What I'm Talkin' About

Go back to the beginning of this chapter and read about Betsy
again.

Decide which "favorite" Betsy was chosen as. Think
about how she'll react and how she'll feel. Imagine what she'll see
next time she looks in the mirror.

Now, the next page, write the story ending, just the way you
see it.

Betsy has come a long way, hasn't she? She isn't the only one.
Right now, you are as beautiful as ...

You!

Betsy's Story Ending...

_____
_____
_____
_____
_____
_____
_____
_____
_____
_____
_____
_____
_____
_____
_____
_____
_____
_____
_____
_____

faithGirlz!

Nancy Rue

EVERYBODY WANTS ME TO
BE MYSELF
BUT I DON'T KNOW WHO I AM

BUILDING
YOUR
SELF ESTEEM

ARE YOU
keeping it real?

4 ARTSY CRAFTS
TO CREATE
YOUR STYLE

WHAT MAKES
youunique?

zonderkidz

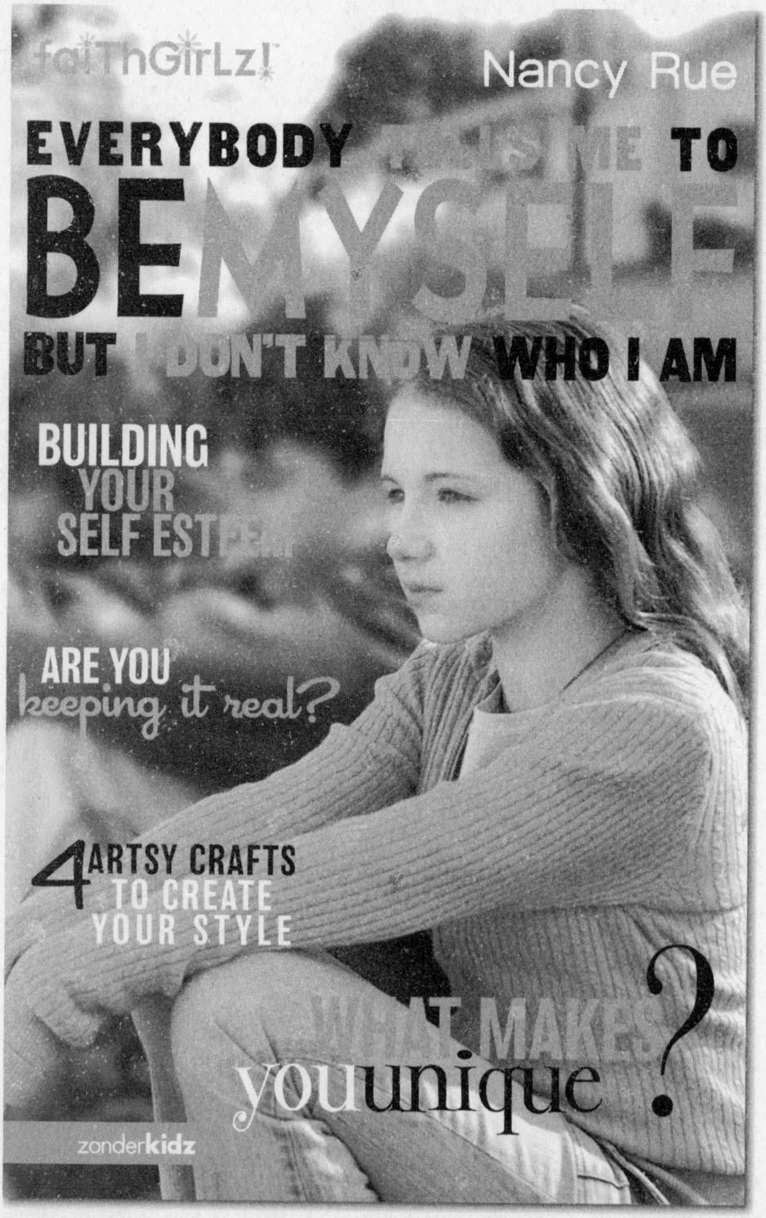

chapter one

Who, ME?

Molly Ann McPherson trailed her fingers over the contents of her brand-new suitcase:

A stack of neatly folded — and very cool — shorts.

Another pile of matching tops, the cutest ever.

A pink zipper bag with her own bottles of everything from shampoo to orange-flavored mouthwash.

And the perfect stationery — shaped like flip-flops — so she could write home every day.

Her summer dream was packed in that suitcase. But suddenly Molly shivered in a blast of cold fear.

"I don't think I want to go to camp, Mom," she said.

Molly's mother looked up at her over the swimsuit from which she was removing the tags. "What?" she said. "All I've heard from you for the last month is how much camp is going to rock."

"But I won't know anybody there," Molly said. "What if everybody thinks I'm a loser? What if I don't make any friends? What if I get left out of everything?"

Molly's mom shook her head. "Don't be silly, Molly," she said. "Just be yourself and you'll be fine."

When her mom left to find the sunscreen, Molly stared miserably at the suitcase full of coolness she'd been so excited about.

Be myself? she thought. *Who's Myself?*

Was she the Molly who was careful to do only what the really popular kids did?

Was she the Molly who always agreed with her friends about every little thing?

Was she the girl who secretly dreamed of being a famous lawyer, or the one who took piano lessons because her mom did when she was a kid, or the one who refused to cry in front of anybody, no matter how sad she was?

Molly slumped on her elbows onto her perfect stacks of camp clothes.

"How am I supposed to be myself," she wailed, "when I don't even know who I am?"

now what?

Poor Molly is having a major case of homesickness, and she hasn't even left her house yet. But there's something else going on too, something that can strike any of us, whether we're thousands of miles from our family or sitting in our own bedroom. It's an attack of the "Who Am I's?" and it can be pretty scary.

The good news is that this book is here to help you

* figure out who you really-deep-down-inside are, and

* be that person no matter who you're with.

It's like a vaccine against future attacks.

Right now we have our Molly, suffering the worst case of the "Who Am I's?" ever. If you were there in the room with Molly and her suitcase, what would you say to her? Would you give her advice? Or would you be absolutely clueless what to say because you feel that same way . . . a lot?

Whatever you want to tell Molly, write it in the space below. There are no right or wrong answers, so be honest. If, as you read the rest of this book, you discover something that makes you change your mind about how to encourage Molly, you'll have a chance to "talk" to her again in the very last chapter.

Dear Molly . . .

Here's the Deal

How many times have *you* heard grown-ups say, "Just be yourself"? Like that's supposed to prepare you for a situation where you don't know anybody, or you don't know what you're supposed to do, or you have that feeling that you are *not* going to fit in at *all*.

In the first place, what do they mean by "be yourself"? They're talking about a thing called *authenticity*. When you're *authentic*,

- ✿ you're completely honest;
- ✿ you don't pretend to be rich, or way smart about something, or totally into horses (or whatever everybody else is into) when you're not;
- ✿ you don't copy the way other kids dress or talk or laugh if it doesn't feel natural to you;
- ✿ you go after the things you're interested in even if nobody else does; and
- ✿ you make up your own mind when it comes to decisions, according to what you know is right and wrong.

That sounds pretty easy, doesn't it? You just do all that stuff and you're authentic.

Yeah, well, if it were that simple, there wouldn't be this book about it, right? Maybe right this very minute you're thinking of one of these problems:

- ✿ What if I'm so honest I hurt people's feelings?
- ✿ What if I just do my thing and everybody thinks I'm weird?
- ✿ What if I always do what's right, and nobody wants to be with me because I'm too "good"?
- ✿ What if I don't even know what I like, and what I'm interested in, and how I want to dress? What about *that*?

Take a big ol' sigh of relief, because this book is here to help you turn every one of those "What Ifs" into a "What Is." You'll learn how to

- ✿ be honest and encouraging at the same time;
- ✿ know what your own "unique thing" is and go for it without caring if other kids think you're weird;
- ✿ show people that "good" is cool; and
- ✿ discover more and more the special, one-of-a-kind person you are... and love you!

Wait... did we just say you're going to love yourself? Isn't that conceited?

Selfish?

Stuck up?

Let's see what God has to say about that.

GOT GOD?

Even if you've only just started thinking about God on your own, you probably know that God-loving people believe God the Creator thought each one of us up, made us, and put us here for a reason. The Bible, where God talks to us, says that over and over. One of the coolest verses is this one:

[God] has shaped each person in turn; now he watches everything we do.
—PSALM 33:15
(THE MESSAGE)

faiThGirLz!

Faithgirlz!—Inner Beauty, Outward Faith

Sophie Series

Written by Nancy Rue

Sophie LaCroix is a girl like you with adventures in her head, and even bigger ones in her real life! With an imagination that both helps *and* gets her into trouble, Sophie's challenges just keep on coming; but her faith keeps growing too. And so will yours, as you get caught up in the story of this sometimes-dreamy-but-ordinary girl with honest questions about God, friends, family, school, and life—and how to make it all work out.

Visit faithgirlz.com, it's the place for girls ages 8-12
Available at your local bookstore!

zonderkidz

faiThGirLz!

Faithgirlz!–Inner Beauty, Outward Faith

Everybody Tells Me to Be Myself But I Don't Know Who I Am

This new addition to the Faithgirlz! line helps girls face the challenges of being their true selves with fun activities, interactive text, and insightful tips.

Everybody Tells Me to By Myself but I Don't Know Who I Am
Softcover, ISBN 0-310-71295-5

My Faithgirlz! Journal This Girl Rocks!

The questions in this new Faithgirlz! journal focus on your life, family, friends, and future. Because your favorites and issues seem to change every day, the same set of questions are repeated in each section. Includes quizzes to promote reflection and stickers to add fun!

My Faithgirlz! Journal
Spiral, ISBN 0-310-71190-8

NIV Faithgirlz! Backpack Bible

The full NIV text in a handy size for girls on the go—for ages 8 and up.

NIV Faithgirlz! Backpack Bible
Periwinkle Italian Duo-Tone™
ISBN 0-310-71012-X

Available at your local bookstore!

faiThGirlz!

Faithgirlz!–Inner Beauty, Outward Faith

No Boys Allowed
Devotions for Girls

Written by Kristi Holl
This short, 90-day devotional for girls ages 10 and up, is written in an upbeat, lively, funny, and tween-friendly way, incorporating the graphic, fast-moving feel of a teen magazine.

Softcover, ISBN 0-310-70718-8

Girlz Rock
Devotions for You

Written by Kristi Holl
In this 90-day devotional, devotions like "Who Am I?" help pave the spiritual walk of life, and the "Girl Talk" feature poses questions that really bring each message home. No matter how bad things get, you can always count on God.

Softcover, ISBN 0-310-70899-0

Chick Chat
More Devotions for Girls

Written by Kristi Holl
This 90-day devotional brings the Bible right into your world and offers lots to learn and think about.

Softcover, ISBN 0-310-71143-6

Shine On, Girl!
Devotions to Keep You Sparkling

Written by Kristi Holl
This 90-day devotional will "totally" help teen girls connect with God, as well as learn his will for their lives.

Softcover, ISBN 0-310-71144-4

Available at your local bookstore!

zonder**kidz**

faiThGirLz!

Faithgirlz!–Inner Beauty, Outward Faith

TNIV Faithgirlz! Bible

Hardcover
ISBN 0-310-71002-2

Faux Fur
ISBN 0-310-71004-9

Faithgirlz! is based on 2 Corinthians 4:38: So we fix our eyes not on what is seen, but on what is unseen. For what is seen is temporary, but what is unseen is eternal (NIV)—and helps girls find Inner Beauty, Outward Faith.

You are totally unique and special—and here's a Bible that says that with Faithgirlz! sparkle.

Features include:

- Dream Girl—use your imagination to put yourself in the story
- Bring It On—take quizzes to really get to know yourself
- Is There a Little _____(Eve, Ruth, Isaiah) in You?—see for yourself what you have in common
- Between You and Me—share what you are learning with a friend
- Oh, I Get it!—find answers to Bible questions you've wondered about
- With TNIV text

... And so much more!

Available at your local bookstore!

zonder**kidz**